I0629841

THE RAIN KING

KEVIN LYNN HELMICK

This is a work of fiction, although places exist and some of the characters have lived and breathed in real life the activities and occurrences in which they are depicted here are entirely of the authors' imagination. It is a novel and not to be confused with actual history.

No part of this book may be reproduced or transmitted in any form without the written permissions of the author and publisher.

Copyright 2014 kevin lynn helmick
All rights reserved.

Isbn 978-0692235829
Isbn 069-2235825

HEARTLAND PRESS
37709 N Delaby Road
Lake Villa IL 60046

THE
RAIN KING

kevin lynn helmick

Dedicated to the spirit and perseverance of independence.

THE RAIN KING

It was like walking into my own funeral. I had never seen so many flowers collected in one place, with all the colliding colors and fragrances and it took some time to gather my senses. They'd crowded in my room to congratulate me on yet another birthday, and they, consisted only of my nurse Jane, Olivia my great granddaughter, and all those flowers. Olivia is the only family I have left. The last of me lies in her.

The red roses were particularly effective, and I asked that those be taken away before my first notion was realized, and they were.

Anyway, they also made an ever bigger to do of it based on the belief that I was one hundred years old. They seemed very certain of this and put it in the newspaper and everything. They brought in a cake with sweet frost; of course I went along with it all.

Olivia even let me have one of her cigarettes, something June never allows. She also slipped two in the pocket of my jacket for later. She is the kindest woman.

I have lived longer than I ever thought or even wanted, and that has made me a lonely stranger in this world. It was nice to be fussed over a bit. It was a good day in such a fragile, questionable world.

You see, I was born into a world very different than the one today, a world wild, unforgiving and its hardships were accepted with a quiet dignity.

Yes, I was born, I lived, I grew old and soon I will die and in that respect I am no different than anyone else. It is the journey of us all. But the world was once a place where men lived and died in a divine synchronicity with nature. It was also a world where you paid the debt of your sins in flesh and blood.

I have known that world.

I have written of these things in my lifetime. A few of you may have noticed.

I made my living telling stories. I wrote and traveled, mostly for newspapers and quarterlies. A few novels and some motion picture writing too. A book about my father sold well enough that I was able to buy a house here in Los Angeles and raise a family. But that was not always my life, and as time takes away all I am now left with just memories and stories. But there is one story that I have never told. I have saved that one for last, a story from my life before.

And although this story makes up a very small part of the time I have spent here, it has consumed me in immeasurable ways. It is a story of happenings between men and Gods. I will dilute the facts in fiction for the sake of entertainment and other reasons, but it is probably mostly true.

My name is George Washington Parker. I am one hundred and seven years old, and this day is not the day of my birth.

All I have left is this memory of a place in time, a certain happening.

And this is the way it goes.

Zelda stood before the sink and watched him through the dirty glass of the kitchen window.

Like a creature void of familiar form his skeletal silhouette stretched across the dry earth and up to the window and there it danced like a black flame in the retina of her straining eye. She furrowed her brow at the shadowed mountains in the distance laying low and sleeping in their ancient beds.

Drying her hands on her thin cotton apron she turned away for just a moment to pull a pan of warm biscuits from the oven and place them on the table. She kissed the burn on her bare fingers and looked out the window again.

He was gone.

She leaned closer to the glass and searched the dead yellowed yard from side to side. But the sun was bright and blinding and all she saw was white and it lingered in her vision after she turned to the darkness inside.

As the room stopped moving she untied her apron, waited for her eyes to adjust and reached for a glass and the bottle of bourbon on the table and poured two fingers. She swallowed it down and poured two more.

The sun light pushed through the windows in dusty yellow shafts creating bright distorted boxes across the red oak floor of the living room. She walked through them like the keeper of a cathedral and made her way to the screen door with the bourbon in hand and stood there for a while. He sat on the top step, shoulders wide and arms on his knees while she watched. His hair, a dirty dish water brown that should have turned gray by now poured from under his wide brim and lay between his shoulder blades.

"Henry."

He didn't answer.

She pushed the screen door open, stepped out and stood next to him. She nudged him with her knee and touched his shoulder with the glass of bourbon. He took it without thanks and set it on the step next to him.

"That's about the end of it Henry," she whispered.

He hated the thought of going into town and pretended he didn't hear.

They both watched yonder as those black hills seduce the sun like they had so many times before and as they would forever. Their faces turned cool and dark in shade of the end of the day. She leaned against the porch rail and looked at the side of his weathered face. "Luck'll turn, always does. Don't worry, it'll come around."

"I know, and I ain't."

He pulled his pipe from the pocket of his trousers and produced a match. He clenched his teeth on the stem and struck the stick across the porch. The flame drew up and he held it out in front of him. It wasn't that he was worried and it wasn't a matter that consisted of luck being either bad or good, but more a feeling of his days stringing together without any real purpose or reason. Every day he would run out of things to do by noon and then drag the rest of the day around behind him like a heavy grudge, and each afternoon it got heavier than the last as the black dog would come to side him and it was in his mind to put him down. He had to and he knew it.

"Supper's ready. Ya want somethin to eat?"

Henry put the flame to bowl and puffed until it glowed and flipped the match away. He reached for the bourbon, poured it down his throat and looked back out across the corrals where a few head of cattle lingered silent and dull. His eyes shifted up to the horizon and he just stayed there. He smoked and stroked his beard from his chin all the way down till his arm once again rested on his knee and his wrist fell limp.

After a long minute she said, "we'll be alright." He hung his head, spit and she stopped talking. In all their years together he couldn't understand her persistence for talk like that. Sometimes she'd even say it to herself.

"I'm fixin to do somethin," he finally said. He spoke in a quiet deep growl and it almost startled her when he did.

"What? What are ya gonna do? It'll come when it comes."

"Yeah… sure wish I could think that a way." He looked back out to the now empty sky turning a night shade of blue.

She shifted her hip and looked out and tried to see what he saw and said, "Are we talkin about the same thing, Henry?"

"I don't know, but I kinda doubt it."

She shook her head as if she understood. "Well, whatever yer talkin bout, I hope it's close nuff."

He took in a deep breath as if to say something that would take lot of breath but just let it out and bit his bottom lip in thought. There was no point in trying to talk it out.

"Alright then," she said turning toward the door. She opened it and stopped. "Supper's ready when you are." And she went inside.

Zee knew her man and she knew when it was best to leave him be. They had been down a long road together but she always felt like she traveled alone.

On the Texas border in a sweat tent there he opened his black eyes and looked about the vision that unfolded from his mind. Parker's breath was steady and controlled as he watched it all like a dream. From high above he hunted the land, the sky, the prairie, the forest with wings full of wind. A village came into view and all the people were leaving, walking in a single file out a southward road to a bridge over a slow river. He stayed and watched as the town emptied.

At the far end came a rider from the west dressed in black on a white horse, lazily lumbering and its shadow cast long and narrow down the street. He watched this man, who seemed to travel but barely move. He was home but lost, here but away, no origin and no destination. Titled and unnamed. He knew this long rider for what he was.

Parker returned after a while leaving the town behind and crossing the wheat and over the forest, across the high prairie and into the desert and back to his tent where his body sat. He felt the heat of the fire there as it lapped and danced, and reached for a gourd taking a mouthful of water and spitting it in the flames he read the smoke. He lifted his medicine sacked and pulled it open and shook it, spilling the tiny bones in the dust on the floor and he read them too.

He shifted his eyes about the walls of the tent, stood and draped himself in a mule deer hide and opened the flap. His eldest son stood crouched and waiting and not a word was passed between them. Parker nodded and the young man mounted his horse and rode north with a selected party.

Parker watched the sun melt across the horizon and shook his head thinking.

Henry Faro was never much of a rancher. He knew horses and cattle but in a different way. He was a soldier once and always. A guerilla fighter and that's where his skills were greatest. He had fought for the south but when the south fell he had fallen with it, far and hard.

War as a boy and back a man and all notions of anything else in his world were weak and dream like. He brought the war back with him like a hungry dog with dry bone. There wasn't much else he knew.

There was something wrong about living past your time he thought. Surviving a war wasn't a good thing. Fighters were supposed to die fighting. Now he spent his years watching over a herd yet to yield, a life yet to hold, a price yet to pay, a failure but with reason and he knew the reason why and it had nothing to do with winning or losing. This life was infinitely harder.

He knew what was coming too, and it wasn't the rain, at least not the kind they needed.

He stroked his beard again, closed his eyes and images flashed in his mind of running horses, hoof beat like the drums of hell for deliverers of death, swift, sure and with extreme prejudice. Gun powder flashes and smoke filled forest. Hot summers and hard winters were as much an enemy as any other. The deafening sounds of dual pistols firing, over and over until the barrels were nearly red hot and tempered. Scenes drenched with torn flesh, dust, blood and fire. He took a deep breath through his nose and the putrid smells of death filled his senses. His heart beat slow and remained calm in his chest. He rubbed the nub of his missing finger.

Phantom pains.

He opened his eyes and scanned the darkening sky. So dark now that the only horizon line was where the blanket of stars stopped and draped behind the range. If he had fallen asleep and woke in another world it would have been fine, but he hadn't. He struck another match and lit his pipe again.

Pulling himself up from the step he walked across the porch catching the screen door behind him and letting it close without a sound. She had turned the lamp up and the fire too, and had taken a seat in an ornamental rocking chair in the corner and pretended to read. She watched him over the top of a King James Bible she had owned since a child. He walked to the kitchen and sat, shuffled his feet and looked at the steak, gravy and biscuits with an insatiable hunger, getting cold. He set his pipe on the table, pulled his pocket watch and checked the time. It was too early for bed but he was tired anyway.

He sat for a while and thought. Days of quick decisions were far behind and time seemed to stand still.

When they moved west from Missouri, they had come in good standing. They had money then for Henry and a few others from the war had banded together and taken to outlawing. They would apply their profession to a more reliable cause, soldiers still, but soldiers of fortune.

And they had the finest clothes, mingled with the upper-class. He presented himself as a horse trader, cattle baron and real estate investor and some considered him only as an anonymous man of importance. He was good at it and there was no fight to it. The capitol he used and where it came from was well known but no one questioned. He was well liked and just as feared. Not till he turned to an honest trade did the money dry up and the fight came to him and it was fight he couldn't win; a fight without purpose, beginning or end, a fight with nature and all her deceptions, a fight with God and all of his.

It had been ten years since he'd bought the ranch and it felt like he'd bought his own prison.

Fidgeting and restless he watched her there in the corner behind her leather bound story book. Her chair squeaked from drought as she rocked. He silently cursed and wondered why she bothered with that old tired thing. His deep eye sockets too dark for her to see, but she could feel his gaze and she placed a toe out, stopped rocking, stopped squeaking, turned a page and pretended it was alright. Zee was a good woman and stood by him always.

He stood up and slid off his coat and hat, walked over and hung them on a peg by the door. He stood for a minute brushing the sleeves while she watched. He walked across the floor to the stairs and began to ascend as she closed the book and set it on the table. His back soon disappeared into the dark along with the sounds of his boot steps.

A door closed.

She looked out the window at the blackness there, shook her head, rubbed her calloused hands together and began a silent prayer that was familiar, memorized and saved for occasions like these and just for Henry. But somewhere in the back of her mind she always suspected it was wasted. For without faith, prayer is just begging.

In the dark on the edge of the bed Henry sat for a long time before he pulled his boots and lay down. He folded his hands behind his head and was in a light sleep before she came. She undressed and watched him breath silent and shallow before she turned the lamp down and fluffed her pillow and worried what to say, what to do.

She woke him in the night carefully, without words and like young strangers finding one another in a vast crowd they made love, quiet and slow.

Dreams filled his sleep and he laid still and watched. One part of his mind tried to wake him but another tried to unravel, tried to stay there and see what would happen. He reached up and rubbed his brow as his eyes moved about under their lids and took dictation of all that was going on. He often dreamt in a certain way, as a curious spectator, hiding, unaffected or removed. But this was different. He was keenly aware that he was the one being watched and found and the dream was coming toward him.

It was not yet dawn when he woke alone. He put his hand in the soft cotton sheets were she'd laid. Still warm.

He swung his feet to the floor and sat rubbing his eyes. He stood, dressed and lumbered to the closet and pulled on his riding boots. He slipped out of the bedroom and walked down the hall with the lantern in hand and stood before a mirror at the top of the stairs. He looked at his reflection next to the flame on the glass for a while and proceeded downstairs to the pantry off the kitchen. He set the lamp aside next to a wash basin and pulled a pair of scissors from a stone jar. Long and sharp the flame from the lamp reflected and poured down the edge or the blades and off the tip. He thought he heard her and tilted his head in that direction, just the never ending wind.

He locked his fingers in the shears, opened them wide and filled them with his beard against the side of his cheek and began to cut. He finished up with a straight razor and felt his neck and chin for stubble missed. Cupping his hands in the cool water of the basin he washed, combed his hair back with his fingers and reached for a folded flannel in the dark of the shelves behind him and patted his face and neck. He turned it in his hand a few times and refolded it putting it back on the shelf exactly the way it was.

When he walked into the kitchen a fire had been made and a coffee pot warmed on the hearth. She sat in the same chair as before with her hands crossed in her lap and her hair mussed from sleep. A cotton bag sat upright on the table where supper the night before had been cleared as if it was never there. He went to a cabinet and pulled out a small flour sack that held bank notes, silver and gold. She watched as he counted the coins and associated them with days, weeks, months and put them all back in the sack and closed the cabinet.

The sun was beginning to rise and he stood before her while she searched him. His clean shaven face had revealed a man that had not aged much in thirty years and the oddity in that made it hard for her to look upon him.

He wanted no coffee but grabbed a cup out of respect and walked over to her and filled it. He sat on the hearth next to her and sipped.

"When will you be back?" she said.

He nodded his head.

"What about..."

"There ain't no what about."

She took a deep breath and pulled her eyes away and they sat there in silence, waiting for the other and finally he broke. "Had a dream in the night."

She didn't want to hear it but she knew he'd tell it anyway.

"There was a bridge, up there above me off to the side." He paused, holding his hand up and spread out for a long time as he recalled. "People, hundreds, maybe even thousands, and they all standin there screamin, cryin and lookin down. I could smell grass and hear the river flowin, cattails swayin in the breeze above me agin a blue sky and I just looked at em, those faces. I don't know what to make of it."

"Sounds awful, like a nightmare," she said.

"Yeah, maybe so."

"Henry, I read once that a bad dream means somethin goods comin, and good dream mean somethin bad."

He took a sip of the coffee. It was bitter and strong. "I heard talk like that too."

"You believe it?"

He looked at her soft eyes growing old and searching for what they wanted. Her pink lips still full but growing little cracks at the corners yet he could still see the little girl in there. He nodded his head at her and said. "I don't believe I do."

Defeated, she took a desperate trembling breath and tried to keep from crying as her eyes closed and her mind fought for something to hang on to, something else she'd read or heard before. Anything to comfort and keep him but she found nothing but dust and dark corners.

It was useless; she knew but said it anyway. "Henry, there must be another way."

He set the cup on the hearth and pushed off his knees and stood. He leaned over and kissed the top of her head and stroked her hair and walked to the large floor safe in the corner. He spun the dial back and forth and pulled the lever and opened the door. Inside were a gun belt rig with two Colt Dragoons and a belt full with brass and lead. He pulled it out and wrapped it around his waist and pulled the buckle tight and pushed the gun buts down on his hips. He picked an immense bowie knife with a clipped sheath that he set and fastened in the nap of his back. He lifted his rifle which he filled with cartridges one by one and leaned it against the wall and another shoulder belt of ammunition. He swung it over his head and it fit and rested comfortable there like it belonged.

He gripped the side by side shot gun, loaded the barrels and closed it. He looked at Zee, nodded and put it back in the safe and left the door open.

She quietly bit her nails in the corner. Her husband the horse and cattleman, the rancher, was gone already if he was ever there at all and in his place stood a figure from the past, a figure of dread and death.

He walked to the coat rack and creaked of leather as he pulled on his coat, split in the back and it draped to just above the knee, fashioned for hiding pistols. He would wear a different hat now; a short stove pipe made of muskrat, dusty and torn and he pulled it down to his brow. His hair long and stringy lay on his lapels and he turned to the sack on the table. He walked over, opened it and shook the biscuits and jerky and tobacco inside and tied it shut.

"If I ain't back in a week, take the money and go where ya please."

He pulled the band of gold from his finger and placed it there on the table, picked up the sack and walked back for the rifle, gave her a nod of thanks and walked out the door into the cool morning air.

She sat looking at the empty doorway, thinking maybe just maybe, and finally pulled her eyes away and to the table where they ring lay. She breathed in deep and trembled, and let it out slow.

The barn doors swung open wide. His best horse whinnied and kicked at his gate as Henry walked up. Jed was a white mustang with black socks, fast and finer than most and still half wild. Henry had been offered small fortunes for his ownership and had declined every one.

Jed looked him over and Henry said. "What ya lookin at?"

Well, looky there, Jed said. Is that Henry? I believe it is. And he's all gussied up for town.

"Shut up."

Even shaved.

He bridled the horse while he snorted and reared. He flung open the gate and led him to the water trough while he outfitted him with blanket and saddle and bed role. Jed drank till he was full and looked at Henry. Where we going, Texas?

"No."

Ya know what they say bout Texas...

Henry cinched the belt tight under Jed's belly. "I do not."

They say it's a nice place to live but ya wouldn't wanna visit.

Henry stood up and looked at the horse. "That don't even make sense. They don't say that."

I've heard it.

"No," Henry spit off to the side and shook his head at the ground, "ya didn't."

She watched him from the porch now leaning against the doorway. Her arms tied across a heavy heart.

Jed stepped back from the water and pulled hard on the reins. Henry jerked his head down with assertion. The horse reared up on his hind quarters as Henry put a boot in stirrup and mounted. They turned in wild quarter circles and left the barn at a full gallop across the yard, past the corral and into the rising sun east.

Zee walked to the corner of the house, leaned over the porch rail, shielded her eyes and watched till their dust was but a memory.

The children had gone to school in the east, two girls, and it had left an uneasy silence behind. And now long lonely uncertain days lay ahead. Would she ever see him again? Would she ever see her children again? She didn't know.

They never wrote.

She went back in the house and stood at the kitchen sink looking out the window and took the last of the bourbon and pulled the cork and drank till it was gone. She broke the bottle in the sink and cut a finger. She watched as the blood filled her palm and she began to cry.

He was named Bird by his mother and it held up over the Christian name his father had given him, his skin a shade lighter and his stature taller than the others but all Comanche in heart. He had not slept but watched the stars and constellation move over his scouting party as they did. And after a breakfast of dog and flat bread the nine of them mounted up on the bare backs of their horses and continued a moderate pace north. He was seventeen years aged and was as much an oddity to the others as his father. His medicine was strong and his disposition serious.

His men were like appendages following his wishes with mere thoughts, gestures and silent glances as they rode across the deserted lower plains without saying a word in the cool dry morning air. He had earned his place before them through competitions of bravery and being the son of his father but he had never seen battle. His mind was clean of the filth of war.

Henry reached town by early afternoon and the streets were busy with barkers and carpetbaggers with goods and trades for sale. Shoppers and workers moved about the planked storefronts while no-gooders slept in the alleys and gutters. He passed the saloon and whorehouse and looked up to the windows were the soiled doves sat yawning and tossing tired waves. He kept on to the stables and stopped. A young boy with bushy red hair and freckles limped out of the darkness on a wooden leg and looked up at Henry and shaded his eyes from the sun with a dirty hand. "Afternoon Mr. Faro," he said.

Henry sat Jed, stepped down and handed over the reins to the boy. "A re-shoe an brush him down good."

"Yessir. Got some fresh grain in, no extra."

"Much obliged," Henry said and pitched the boy a silver dollar.

"I'll wash him too."

Henry looked at Jed and could see his grin. "I recon he'd like that."

The boy bit the coin between his teeth and when he looked up Henry was gone.

In the sun he leaned against a porch post outside the cafe and rolled a cigarette while a small crowd gathered around a horseless carriage chugging steam in the street. He lit and watched the folks feet scurry about under the clouded calamity. He knew Jed was suspicious of these contraptions and so was he.

"Somethin else, ain't it?" Sherriff Olson yelled from the doorway behind. "Times a changin."

"Need to shout to think," Henry said without turning around.

"What's that?"

Henry spit and Olson understood. "Come on inside, Henry. Buy ya cup."

Olson was a large smiling man and cheerful always even when he killed. They had known each other since the war. Henry turned, followed him and closed the door but it did little for the noise. They took a table in the back as far away as they could. The smell of bacon burned from the kitchen and filled the café with a dense haze. Olson sat and said, "lost yer beard Henry."

"I know where it is." Henry replied placing his hat on the table and taking the chair across facing the door.

"I reckon ya do." Olson waved over the obese waitress and she squeezed her way sideways through the tables and chairs. Her black hair was wrapped around the top of her head like a hat of great effort. "Tilly honey, could ya put a fresh pot on for my friend here?"

"Sure Sherriff. Would the gentleman like somethin to eat?"

"Ya wanna eat Henry?" Olson raised his eyebrows and grinned. "Tilly makes a mean biscuit."

"Coffee's fine," he said, even though he wanted nothing really but to talk.

Tilly maneuvered her way back through to the kitchen and screamed something incoherently at the cook.

Olson leaned forward and whispered, "you could lose a tooth on those biscuits a hers. Good call."

Henry smiled a little.

"Hey, Lucy's got a new a girl in last week from back east, real purty too and right friendly at that."

"Last week?"

"Yeah, well," Olson laughed. "New enough for Lucy's place I guess. And the railroaders don't get off till dark so, doubt if anybody's had her today. She'll clean yer bone damn good she will."

Henry looked out the windows there. The steam car had quit or gone on and the sounds of the town came forward. The clank of hammers sinking spikes in the rails far off, women cackling like chickens in the street and the sounds of hoofs on the earth while wagons rattled and creaked by. "It's a thought," he said without putting much into it.

Olson chewed on Henry's appearance awhile and finally asked, "why ya packin, Henry? Hardly recognized ya at first glance. Thought ya's one them bounty hunters driftin through."

Henry pulled himself around and picked up a spoon from the table and looked at the odd reflection it gave. "I'm headed up east on some business. I'd like it if you'd ride out, check on Zee in a day or two if I ain't back by then."

"Business ya say, back east?'

"Yep."

Olson wanted more but decided not to pry on it for what might come out. "Sure, I'd do that. But ya know I never met the woman. She know I'm comin?"

"Nope. Good chance ya won't need to though. Just in case. Bring her some whisky, flour, some a that hard candy from the store."

"I reckon that'd help." He said looking at Henry sideways.

"Don't worry, she won't shoot ya. Probably she won't."

"That's reassuring, Henry."

Tilly came back with the coffee and two mugs and slammed them down on table. She looked at the side of Henry's face as she poured and looked at the Sheriff when she was done. He just nodded a cautionary no, and she walked away to the side of the room and sat at her table there and began folding the linens in exhausted exasperated motions.

Parker lulled about the ranch all morning. He leaned on the fence of the corral and watched the horses there as if in conversation. He drank from the well and split some wood, which he never did before and all watched with apprehension as if they failed him in some way.

He changed his clothes twice and bathed in between in the morning sun while two of his wives washed him clean. He walked out far west of the house and sat cross legged looking back for long periods of time and then he walked to the east and did the same. His wives, children and workers were uneasy of his behavior and tried not to look or loaf under his gaze. There had been a certain stillness in air since Bird and his party headed north and that stillness became heavier as the sun rose and the shadows hid from the heat in the hours that passed.

A wolf lingered a half a mile south of the property, bold, rabid and he eyed the ranch but came no closer. As if a wall stood in the way it paced back and forth around the perimeter and watched Parker do the same. At some point to one of the more astute children it became apparent that they were engaged in some sort of dance, his father and that wolf.

When the afternoon passed Parker crossed his arms and walked back toward the house while speaking words never written by man. The wolf loped silently away fading into a mirage to the west.

Henry left Olson and the café through the back and made his way to Lucy's saloon. Olson and Tilly sat stealing glance across the room at one another as Henry's coffee stayed untouched between them. Lucy was leaning back in her chair at the far end of the bar smoking a corncob pipe when Henry entered from out of the shadows of the balconies in the back. She was nearly seventy and could have easily been mistaken for a man though even older.

Her flannels britches the color of ash held up by red suspenders over a denim button down. She coughed and spit on the floor to her side when Henry stepped up to bar. "What a ya have, Henry?" She wore a toothless grin and the gleam in her eyes shined like distant stars through a clouded sky.

Henry turned and saw her sitting there in the empty room. She nearly blended out of sight except for her straw hat with a dead rose tucked in the band. "Bottle and a whore," he said.

Lucy let a raspy laugh that turned into a choking fit while Henry watched. When she gathered herself to a standing position she moved behind the bar not taking her eyes off Henry. "Mighty early for a rancher."

Henry pursed his lips and shrugged. "Some might say, mighty late."

She pulled a bottle off the shelf behind and slid it down the rail and agreed. "Some might say that."

"I heard ya had new girl."

She dusted off a glass with a dirty bandana and offered it up to Henry. He took it and the bottle and stepped back and waited for her reply. She chewed on her pipe and said, "top a the stairs, last door on the left."

"Much obliged," Henry said and turned away.

"Sure yer up for it old man?"

Henry placed a boot on the first step and looked over.

"She's a handful, this un."

He paused, thought it through and continued up the stairs while the old woman laughed and shook her head.

He got to the top and looked back at Lucy below who broke into a jig and laughed waving him on.

He walked to the end of the hall and stood outside the door and listened. She hummed a song in there he'd hear before and he knocked with the toe of his boot.

The door flew open with a gust. She stood naked and barefoot, except for the dirty white stockings that pinched her tiny thighs, smiling with enthusiasm as if she'd been waiting for Christmas morning and it was finally here. She was pretty, with a pile of yellow curls pinned here and there.

She backed away and beckoned him with her index finger and blue eyes while throwing herself on the bed. Henry stood in the doorway and watched as she began rubbing herself there.

He stepped in, closed the door with the heel of his boot and said, "How ya doin, girl?"

She rolled her head back in the sheets and gasped in pleasure as the tips of her fingers disappeared between her legs up to large glass ring she wore that pushed and rotated against her knuckle.

He wondered what she did on her time off but the answer was clear. There was no time off for this one.

She pulled her hand out and launched herself off the bed and onto Henry, wrapping her legs around his waist. She touched his lips with that hand. He could smell her and he began to grow.

"I'm Lily," she said.

She smiled a smile that men kill and die for.

"Lily."

He turned away from her gaze; he had to, setting the glass and bottle on the night stand. He pulled the cork while she dropped to her knees and pulled at his buckles and rubbed her hands over his guns while he poured. She was not a patient girl and Henry was grateful not to have to work at it. There would be no need for fancy talk and manners.

She pulled it out and caught the smells of Zee still there from the night before and looked up at Henry. "Ya been a busy boy," she said and laughed.

Henry held his glass up and poured it down.

Little Lily went to work on him.

Henry stayed the afternoon and into the night while the saloon filled with angry patrons bringing gifts of flowers, perfumes and other frailties for their true love Lily. They waited with ears pressed outside her door, drank and pouted at the bar while their hopes faded further away with each passing hour.

Bird made camp the same night on a wide savannah. They hunted rabbits and made a small fire and the fat one they called Churro sat near Bird and said in Comanche, "It has been a long time since we hunted together. It is good and fills me with memories."

Churro knew this was no hunting trip for most of the men were older and warriors and not known to hunt. Although capable, they were used to having their meals prepared for them. Bird looked at Churro and back into the fire.

"It is a beautiful night and a good one to be alive and witness," Churro said looking up at the heavens above, and then he looked at a Bird a long minute before answering himself. "Yes Churro, It is a beautiful sky and I am proud to be here with a hunter as fine and good as you."

Bird smiled and glanced only briefly at his friend and shook his head.

"Well, are you going to tell me what we are doing out here? I have a warm bed and a wife who likes to make babies."

"Her sister too," Bird said.

"You have been spying on me?"

"No, it is well known."

"Tell me where we are going. What has that crazy father of yours dreamed?"

Bird shook his head and smiled a coy smile.

"You don't know either, do you? That is why you won't tell me."

"I will not tell you, Churro because it is not something that concerns you. You are here to hunt rabbits and feed the men. And if you get to miss your wife and her sister too much, well, I will let the men share you if it will keep you warm and quiet."

Churro's jaw stiffened and he spit and cursed under his breath as he rolled to his feet and stomped away. Bird could hear laughter in the dark.

Henry rode along the border of Kansas and away from the Oklahoma territory he called home, a casual traveler through no man's land. Herds of horses ran wild far out to his right side and in his flank. They seem to know more than any man could. Thousands of them there on the high grassy plain that probably wondered up from the ranch of Parker, the half breed Comanche warrior turned statesman, the buffalo now all but gone.

White clouds thin as smoke would appear and disappear from time to time as the sun passed over and behind.

It would be storm season soon and the funnels would come and sweep across this land in groups and take what they wished without care or mercy and no prayer was ever written or spoken that could persuade them otherwise. The land needed rain but it would pay a high price.

He passed through small towns, barely more than camps, where tired faces looked up without expression or greeting and they watched as he came from a long distance and he could still feel them watching even as he was miles out of sight.

He thought about many things as a man does on a long journey. The hours and miles passed with little notice and the world seemed small. He remembered a time when that wasn't so and he couldn't decide which was true if either.

He came to the eastern timbers and when the time was right headed north into the wheat fields of Kansas toward a small town he knew as Independence.

He camped that night two miles out on the edge of a river in a grove of cottonwoods and ate biscuits and jerky while Jed watered himself and grazed on the grass there. He could see a bridge far down river and watched it often but no one crossed. He smoked his pipe by the fire and thought of her and what she'd be doing under the same moon. The stars were such that there was barely room for one more. There was a cool quiet comfort in the air.

Henry didn't sleep. Instead he sat and stared into the fire and prepared his skills long dulled. He scouted the perimeter and brushed his hands across the tips of the grasses and listened to the way the breeze made it rustle and hush. He talked to Jed in a kind whisper of the things that horses dream of. Jed said, some men were born to sit by a river and Henry agreed that on a night like that it would be a good enough reason to live.

The night veiled the present and soft memories came and went with the waters slow current

He sharpened his knife on a stone by the bank and cleaned his guns and when the sun colored the eastern sky warm with the promise of morning he re saddled Jed, drank coffee, broke camp and they waded across the river in the shallows.

He thought he'd recognized the bridge downstream now. He convinced himself that it was only from the dream, just a picture from his mind's eye but still it pulled on him as a place of some importance.

He had crossed many bridges in his life he thought, and put this one with the rest and rode on.

They gathered there in streets, quiet, methodic and somber. All walked in the same direction to the south end of town like cattle being herded by some silent shepherd. Barely a greeting was made on this summer morning and all dressed in their finest clothes while the sun rose and the birds watched from ridges high.

A chugging steam wagon came around a corner adorned with white silk draped from its buck boards and from a rocking chair throne nailed in back, he rode and waved a blessed hand as he passed each one. The horseless carriage sputtered, swerved and spun dust as the driver, a young boy, bit his lip and fought to keep this difficult machine in the street. The man would smack his shoulder with long staff, left and right as if steering a mule through the small crowd and they parted and watched them speed by as the dust soiled their clothing and caked their hair.

Along the narrow dirt road out of town they followed and talked quietly among themselves and brushed the dust from one another. Men good and backward, shop keepers and farmers, women, mothers, cooks, sowers and social planners, and they all moved along to their morning service.

As Henry crested an easy hill, lush and green on the edge of town, there stood a great white tent like a swollen blister rising from the prairie floor surrounded by trodden down grasses.

The last few figures approached and were swallowed up by a slit in the side. The strange horseless wagon sat and chugged stream in the breeze. A few horses gathered but to the far end and away from the strange carriage. Several wandering dogs there doing the things that dogs do.

The morning sun reflected off the massive tent and caused it to glow like the salvation within was real and alive. Henry knew it as makeshift church, a circus of souls. "Ya ever seen a thing like that?"

Jed said no, but that he had not seen everything in the world.

Henry agreed that he had not either, but knew in fact, the dry plains were thick with these sky grifters. He had seen and heard of their doings before.

He trotted up slow and once they were there he pulled Jed down to a walk and slipped on by. Two dogs watched while fucking and did not stop as Henry passed. The other dogs watched too and some cowered around out of sight but none bothered to bark at the lone stranger.

I never liked dogs much, Jed said.

"I reckon they don't like you much neither."

Look at em there.

"Yer just jealous."

What is, jealous?

"Never mind, quiet down."

As they rode past Henry could hear the sermon inside and the results in the affected through their crying cheers. The screams of new born babies broke the morning and filled the air. The whole town must have needed saved he figured from the sounds of it. Jed snorted nervously and wanted to run. Henry felt the same but kept at a casual quiet pace and on into town.

Passing the first of a row of houses, stately Victorian's and Heartland Gothic's, they walked down Main Street. His figure in black on a mostly white horse on an otherwise perfect sun drenched morning was as out of place and added eeriness to the silence.

Not a sound or soul, save for the sparrows and crows that came to them as they passed the dry goods, blacksmiths and livery stables. Jed's hoofs thumped the ground and echoed off the buildings as they walked.

A grand hotel stood two decks high in the center of town, dirty, dingy and badly in need of paint, across from The Independence Savings and Loan.

He didn't look that way but rode between the hotel and a cafe, double backed and crossed over and tied off behind the bank. There was not one saloon along the streets that he could remember passing.

Henry stepped off, pulled his watch and checked the time, untied a saddle bag and slung it over his shoulder as Jed watched him walk away with intelligent curiosity.

I think we should talk about this, Jed said. Think it over some breakfast.

"It'll be alright. I've been thinking about it for some time and nothings come of that."

Just sayin.

"I know. And you can just stop that."

He started to walk away and Jed said, two hunert thousand die every day.

Henry turned and looked at the horse. "Now why would ya go and say a fool thing like that?

I don't know.

"I think yer math is wrong. I think it's probably more."

I figure numbers good. I don't why.

"I... just shut the hell up," he said and walked away. "Yer givin me the willies talkin like that."

Henry stopped in the shade at the corner of the bank and stood for a moment and scouted the windows and doors across the street. "Goddamn horse."

He stepped up on the boardwalk and through the doors and stopped. A box of complimentary cigars sat on a small writing podium and Henry took two, putting one inside his coat and the other to his teeth where he bit the end and spit.

"Morning stranger," the young man called from behind the gilded teller cage. He smiled and pushed his spectacles tight with his fore finger.

Henry looked at him and reached in his pocket for a match and struck it ablaze with his fingernail. He pulled the flame into the cigar and puffed until it was well lit. The young man fidgeted nervously as Henry stepped up. "Well, good mornin to you son," Henry said grinning wide.

The young man smiled and straightened himself. "How can I help you sir?"

"Fixin to do some bankin," Henry said and laid the saddle bag on the counter.

The young man glanced at the leather, swallowed hard and said, "ah, a new account, a deposit?"

Henry smiled pulled his coat behind his pistols. "Not exactly."

The man's face turned white and a bead of sweat balanced on his brow. "I know you. I know who you are. Yer dead, mister. Yer supposed to be, dead."

Henry sniffed a smile and pursed his lips. He leaned closer and studied the man's face, his narrow string tie and his white button down soaking through with sweat. "Put the money in the bag son and I'll be on my way."

"Mister, I can't do that. I just... I can't."

Henry nodded and turned the cigar in his fingers. "What do they call you boy?"

"Phillip, They call me... I mean, my name sir, is Phillip."

"Well, Phillip, do ya want em to call *you*, dead too?"

"No sir, I sure don't want that." Phillip removed his glasses and placed them on the wood before him. They rattled on the oak from his trembling hands.

"Then I believe we can do business." Henry smiled again and winked. "Go on now."

Phillip began to shake his head no and pulled his eyes away. Henry reached between the bars and grabbed Phillip's shirt and pulled his face hard into gilded iron grill and screamed, "Put the money in the fuckin bag, ya goddamn jayhawker." His spit splattered the man's face and he gave his shirt a twist, strangling him. He let off enough to slam the man's face again. "do it now, cocksucker."

"Ok, alright," Phillip said. "I have a child, a wife, Mr.-"

Henry stopped him, "don't you say it, ya son of bitch," and slammed his face into the bars again. The young man was crying now and the bridge of his nose was bleeding. He reached down and produced a wad of crumpled notes and showed them to Henry. Henry let go and pushed the saddlebag forward. He slid a thumb in his watch pocket and puffed the cigar while Phillip filled the bag.

"The Sheriff here... is pretty mean Mr. He'll hunt ya down. He won't stop. No one has ever robbed this bank."

"Is that right?"

"Yes sir. He's the Reverend too, giving his morning sermon right now."

"Reverend, huh, don't say?"

"Gives a sermon every single morning." Phillip finished filling the bag and looked at Henry. "Mister, there are those in our congregation that'd follow him to hell and back."

"To hell and back, ya say?"

"Yes sir."

Henry smiled and winked at Phillip. "There is no back, boy. You talk to fuckin much."

"Oh no sir, Reverend Poole says…"

"Poole?"

Henry knew the name, knew it well, but it seemed like a lifetime ago when he heard it last. "Tell me boy, why ain't you out there with the rest a them ass-holes?"

"The Reverend blessed me, exempt, on a count of the bank and all. Somebody's gotta be here."

"Is that right… zempt, huh?"

"Yes sir, the Reverend…"

"Shut the hell up, boy. I ain't interested in none a that shit."

"You asked…"

"Shut it."

"Yes sir. I…"

"Goddamn it, I told you to shut."

Phillip shut up, nodded and closed the flap on the bag and pushed it over.

"I think you outta know somethin," Henry said. "That man out there, that Reverend a yers, ain't what he says. An his name ain't Poole neither."

Phillips listened but Henry could tell he was wasting his breath.

He grinned and drew a pistol so fast that the black hole smoking in Phillips head was nearly there before he pulled the trigger.

Phillip stared at Henry, dead on his feet and Henry said, "Yer dead boy, lay down now." The young man fell backwards and his feet sprung up from the floor and shook violently to rest. Henry glanced at the blood and brain stain on the wall behind. It was shame he thought, being recognized after all these years and how something like that could be so terminal. He tossed the bag over his shoulder and walked out.

A curtain cracked and fell back in place from an upstairs window of the hotel as Henry rounded the corner and back to Jed. An old woman sat confined to her chair behind the glass and saw all and more.

She began to lay her cards out on the table, one by one. Her shaking fingers, diseased and arthritic snapped them down. She grinned as she read their meaning and began to laugh in a way that she hadn't in a very long time.

Henry saw the movement of the curtain out the corner of his eye but decided in an instant that he was too far away to be described with any real certainty. Jed jumped and snorted. His heart had been quickened by the sound of the gunshot and his eyes were bulged and crazed. He was ready to run.

Two hunert and one, Jed said.

"You want shot?"

No. No I don't. I can figure numbers good though. Why is that?

"Maybe yer cursed."

I think I might be.

Henry knew he asked for that one and sighed, disapproving of the sarcasm.

Pulling the reins from the hitching post he tied the saddle bag off and pulled himself up. They trotted down the back alley. Jed pulled hard and whinnied in defiance with the slow pace but Henry insisted and reached down patting his neck. "Easy, easy. Soon enough, gotta be quiet now."

This was a very bad idea, Jed said as they walked. Don't make no sense.

"I done things that make less sense."

True, true, like when you killed that cat that took up in the barn.

"Shut up."

That cat was all right, kept the mice out.

"Shush, damn it."

What'd that cat do to you?

"Goddamn it." Henry spurred Jed in the flanks and the he let the matter be.

They cut between and behind a few houses to the west and halted on the edge of town before the vast and open grassland where the tent of God stood. Henry watched the grand white elephant for a moment, dreamy and surreal from that distance, flapping in the breeze, glowing in the late morning sun and he wondered about the man within.

He measured the idea of a Reverend Sheriff. It seemed like a contradiction from what he knew of the man. He wondered if the Morning Prayer was a law and taxed as such. He had never met a, man of God, who deserved the title, and had seen too much of hell to put much stock in it.

He glared upon the tent, knowing full well they should be earning distance.

Really? Jed said. We just gonna sit here?

"Shut up."

I take it back, Jed whispered, go ahead and shoot me.

Tinges of horror fell over Henry like he hadn't felt in years. He stared on. He had thought those feelings only had a home in the halls of hell, the deep sleep of war, put to rest in the waking world and only saved for nightmares and day dreams. Instincts that Henry recognized as worthy of attention: that chill up the spine that warned of an assassin near and at work, that silent scream in the stem of the brain that spoke of danger the instant before it arrived, the uneasiness of a bend in the road and the way all of nature would caution life.

Jed felt it too.

God-damn Henry, could we please get outta here?

Henry ignored the horse and narrowed his thoughts in closer.

Many paths cross in the course of a well-traveled life and if destiny demands they must cross again. He bit his bottom lip as he sometimes did when thinking. He knew that man could hold and govern such an assembly. They were bonded in a way. He knew the power of the book too, useless in the hands of his wife but what it could do in the hands of a man like Poole was something else altogether. It was not a feeling of comfort.

Jed knew as any sensible being would and was restless and couldn't understand Henry's fascination and lack of response. He stomped and paced and circled. Two hunert and three, two hunert and four, he said.

"Shut-up."

It's good day for the devil.

"Smartest thing ya said all morning."

The Reverend Livius Poole stood before them now in dirty white from hat to boot, a congress of searchers, believers, lost and weak, and he raised his arms high and walked about the small platform above them all. His long fingers pale and spread, reached to the roof of the large circular tent and he closed his eyes and nodded slowly over the crowd as if counting his flock and they watched with obedience and anticipation. His hair and beard were white as well and took on the striking image of who they all believed he was. He was aglow with a fierce and powerful presence.

"There be sinners at our door." He finally spoke when the time was right and timing was everything in the trade of the Lord. "That of fornication, adultery, and the lust of a whore."

They all gasp wide eyed and looked about. Their contorted faces stretched and some wept and shrieked in disbelief.

"Hear ye, and the Lord sayeth and brings on to me His word and wisdom, a mission delivered unto thee that these sinner be cast free by my hands and through thee to the Lord for cleansing upon which they can be spared of the fires of hell and damnation. So it be. So it be."

He turned his back to the congregation and to a woven basket on the table and opened it. He reached inside and spoke in a whisper a language that held no reasoning with the people who listened save for the conviction in which it was delivered. They struggled to understand and see as he turned wide eyed and teeth clenched.

Snakes rattled, twisted and slithered around each of his massive arms with their heads squeezed between his fists. Their forked tongues lashed about at the air above their heads. They grasped themselves and some fainted to the floor while others looked on.

"He came onto me in an hour of darkness and revealed the names. He bestowed onto me the nature of their games. He gave onto me the powers that are His and for His chosen to be those powers of His land. For crimes committed by and against His children He will not stand. And only by faith can ye be passed into His eternal glory and only by obedience and humility can ye enter upon His kingdom. And only if ye giveth thy soul in the here and now can ye be accepted by His love through me His chosen deliverer of His true and only word can ye enter.

Hear me now, it be the truth and the way, if ye want the rain, then these sinners must be slain."

Some closed their eyes and whispered hallelujah with such acceptance that they knew without doubt or reason that the words were true. Others recited prayers of agreement in meditated consciousness.

Others looked about nervous and with guilt that knotted their souls and tightened their throats.

"I have been sent to ye, for ye have been chosen, but we have been tainted by adultery and we cannot move on to grace until these sins have been spoken for. And ye have been cleansed of the filth of the flesh. Do ye believe?"

They muttered they did, fixed and hypnotized by the stranger that come to them and carried with him all the words they wanted to hear. And a year had passed since they were blessed with his arrival and nearly all had been saved in that time and many had been sent for the cleansing now spoke of and the promise they would live on eternal in His heavens.

"Do ye Believe," he shouted again and passed his snake coiled arms over the tops of their heads and all save one in the back and one in the shadowed side reacted with the shouting that they did, they believed, and they begged and raised their hands in praise and they cried and moaned and swooned in the heat of the holy carnival.

He moved his arms over them and his left arm stopped straight ahead to the back and his right arm stopped pointed to the side and he opened his eyes. "The wages of sin be death, save be all the rest. He commands it, for it be true, for only through death can ye be new." They all looked about dumb faced and slack jawed.

The man in the back looked at his friends and neighbors and made a run for the opening of the tent that he had been inching nearer and nearer to. Deputies in black blocked his way with force and God and loaded guns.

The woman on the side clutched her handkerchief and nodded her head no. "It's a lie," she said. "Please... it's not true." She turned to her husband, stone faced and furious.

"Whore!" He shouted in her face and his spits of hate were her final tears.

"Bring them forth," the reverend said. "Bring them both before the Lord to pay for the evil they have brought from the gates of hell onto God's chosen ones and we shall deliver them into salvation."

And they all converged on the guilty with the hate and anger of a horde wronged. They brought with them a hunger for righteousness and a lust for revenge. And the accused protests of innocence fell under the savage screams and glassy eyes of the Lords fury and they were beaten battered and their limbs torn from their torsos and held in the air like trophies of the insane as the children grimaced and cheered.

And all that was wrong was righted again.

Henry was taken with the screams from the church and finally came around. He didn't need to prod Jed either but let the reins slack a little and Jed bolted, uninterested in all but escape. They ripped through the grass at a speed that was beyond Jed's known stride. Henry looked back over his shoulder at the white monstrosity in its golden bed. Jed did not.

They reached a bank in the field that welcomed a sheltering patch of timber. Paper elms and apple trees in full bloom over bright green grass littered with daisies and other prairie flowers. Henry slowed the horse and ducked through low hanging limbs and pulled a couple apples as they passed and set them in his pockets. Jed was still skittish and resisted resting, fighting Henry's decision to linger.

I don't want no apples, Jed said.

Henry did not speak but sat the horse and looked backed and listened for any sounds beyond that of natural nature.

Did you not hear what went on in there? I did. I don't want any part of that.

"Quiet now," Henry said and watched the horizon from where they came.

Ya ain't gotta prove it to me ya know.

"What's that?"

That you can do things that make lesser sense than the thing before.

Henry let out a sigh and slapped the reigns a little. "I don't intend to."

They crossed the river in a different place than before and rode on through the timber. Henry thought about life again. He couldn't avoid it. It seemed so small from his aging perspective, this life, so many miles, so many dead. So many stories told and untold and yet the truth lay buried somewhere among the roots and shadows of time.

He tried to find it in his mind. Tried to remember where it was, where it was left. It all flooded his memory and swept the day away but nothing was found.

From his earliest recollections and into youth, war and women gone, trails and woods and camps and caves, cities and towns. It seemed like such a long story now, like many lives strung together, an epic tragedy full and heavy with burden and mistakes. Images of friends and family flipped through his mind's eye like a thumbing of the pages of a post mortem picture book.

Maybe it was his advancing years, maybe that's all it was, but Henry was feeling a worry that had never overcome him before. Maybe it was the stillness of the town. Maybe it was the ominous presence of religion and faith that throbbed from the tent. Maybe it was the screams that rang out from inside. Maybe it was guilt, an emotion that often seeds in a life's later years. He veiled and skirted the truths with maybes, but knew in the back of his mind the fact of his worries and it spoke in tongues and distant whispers and the voices were mocking, taunting him.

He had made a very big mistake.

He couldn't let go the picture of that canvas church in his mind and it lingered like a dream, silent and misty. He thought about it and the man inside for the rest of the day.

But as night fell his worry weakened with distance and as time feeds the bold he started thinking of the ranch and business life again. A trip down to Texas for cattle and horses, some much needed repairs. Maybe sell it all and on to California for a city life, open a public house, a newspaper. Zee would like that.

San Francisco.

They had spent their honeymoon there during a warm winter in seventy two and it was a good memory.

A night bird called from the shadows of a pine yonder. He could hear it now it and its song was one of the present and it brought him back and saddened away his dreams of a future.

Jed pulled on the reins and said, look at there.

Henry looked up to a figure on the dark road in the distance, horseless and wavering like a drunkard from side to side. They stopped and the man kept coming in their direction. He wore an infantry coat, northern but faded past the point of any real color. One boot soul flapped like a coloreds lips as he walked and it spoke of hardship and a road near its end.

He was old, older than Henry. His hair and beard were silver and nearly matched the color of the rest of him, covered in dust. He looked as if he'd been walking since the war, forty years and more and whatever home he had before then was lost too him now.

Closer he came with his heavy head down and would have walked right into them if Jed hadn't reared and stepped back.

"Who's there," he shouted and turned an ear.

"What are ya doin out here old man?"

The man raised his head; eyes cinched tight as if stitched by a doll maker and said, "Who?"

Henry looked around and behind him up the trail. "You blind..."

"I ain't blind. Yer blind. Ya sons a bitch."

He started to walk past. "Hold on there," Henry said.

"Leave me be goddamn it. War's over." He raised his hands and started to feel his way around them.

Henry pulled and cocked a pistol, turned Jed around in the road and Jed said, here we go.

"Hold on old man," Henry said.

The old man stopped, and turned his head to the side. "Fuck you. Fuck ya all to hell. Gonna shoot me cocksucker? Go on then, get it done."

Henry bit his bottom lip and held his weapon at arm's length. "Where in the hell ya goin?"

The old man turned all the way around now and laid his dirty fingers on his hips, cut and bloody from limbs and thorns. "That ain't none a yer business, mister."

"Look," Henry said lowering his pistol. "I got some water here, some jerk, you hungry?"

The old man furrowed his brow and cocked his head as if hearing something far away, and then let out a grunt. "Jerk?" He thought it through. "Fuck off. Leave me be." He turned and went on his way.

Henry watched for a long time as the man eventually wondered off the path and back into the woods. Jed stood and waited.

"What do ya make a that?"

Jed rattled his bridle. I don't make nothin a that, just some no eyed nut.

They continued on and Henry was grateful for something else to think about.

"I saw his face clear as the glass in that winder," she said. "Saw him walk in, heard the shot and when he walked out there's not a doubt in a mind, is him alright."

The Reverend stood in the window and looked across the street at the bank. He turned and faced her and the setting sun cast a holy glow around his figure. Her wheel chair creaked as she straightened the pleats of her dress and sat herself up on skeletal arms.

"Ye say ye seen this man that all have known to be long dead, ye saw a ghost I say, a demon."

"Wudn't no ghost, no demon. We's all from the same parts. Swears God, it was him. Cept-"

"Except what?"

"Cept he looked the same, looked young like back when we knew em all em years go." She coughed and spat on the floor and Poole's lip curled. "Swears to God," she added.

"Swears God." Poole nodded to the floor.

He walked toward her and kneeled before the crippled old woman and took her by the soft hand and rubbed it and looked at the lines on her palm. "Lyin an swearin in the name of the Lord is a sin,

Mae Beth. You may have been deceived by your diseased soul."

"I saw him Reverend. I'd know him anywheres. Is him alright. As sure as I's sittin here."

He looked at the tarot cards on her table. He knew these cards. Cards of Satan's, laid out in configured applications. The death card lay atop face up and called to the Reverend. He clenched her withered hand until the pain reached her eyes. Her toothless mouth gaped. Her breath quickened and she fought from crying. "Please, no."

He put his face close to hers. "Could it be your witchery conjured this demon?" He eyed his deputy William Rhoar standing silent and hands folded before him by the door. Rhoar nodded and left the room.

A panic swept over her face as she watched the door close and latch. Poole loosened his grip and slid his fingers between hers.

Rhoar stood in the hall and listened.

"No, Reverend. No sir. Since ya came I seen the light. I only keepin watch so's this tired ole sinner might be a some use. Please," she said and a single tear followed down a long deep wrinkle to her chin where it dropped. Poole caught it in his palm and rubbed it away.

"I see. But ye work here is done. Ye have no use in this world or the next," he whispered and stood and kicked the table over. He looked at the tarot cards and the way they landed. He reached down and picked one of no particular meaning to him and waved it in the air as if relieving a foul smell before spinning it into her lap.

She looked down at the card. "I been saved, Reverend. Thanks to ya'll I knowd the wrong I'd done and the days God has left me with will all be spent grateful like. I swear it."

He walked around the back of her chair and stood looking at the top of her head. He pursed his lips and shook his head. He lifted a black silk scarf from the backrest of her wheelchair and wrapped it around his fists. "Ye have done well in that service, Mae. And the Lord has spoken for thee to come home I say. But what did the cards tell ye?"

She waved her hand in the air and shook her head. "They don't mean nothin, fools game."

"What did they say," he said again and dropped the scarf over her head from behind and let it lay across her sunken breast as a warning.

She knew. Her brow wrinkled and came to a point on her forehead. "They say he's a gonna kill you, you sons a bitch."

She looked out the window filled with light and trembled and closed her eyes and remembered the things she had loved in her life. He pulled the scarf tight around her neck and he lifted and prayed in a bellowing voice to the dirty ceiling while she spit and cursed him. Her fingers clawed at the air until they too fell as limp as the rest of her broken body. And she was dead.

"So it be," he said and wiped his brow with the scarf and slipped it into his pocket. He kneeled and fascinated at the cards on the floor for a while before standing and walking out.

The Moon had not yet risen when they topped a hill at the edge of the woods. Suddenly the world opened up to a vast mesa dotted with black patches on the yellow floor. It reminded Henry of a leopard he saw once in a Wild West show in Kansas City. A breeze picked up and carried with it a stench, familiar and belonging to only one thing on earth.

Jed said, let's take another trail.

He tried to focus his eyes in the dark. The chill that had settled in was not from the night. They walked down the hill and Henry was forced to pull his bandana up and cover his breath. Jed jerked his head and tried to lead off and away. But Henry forced him up to the nearest carcass.

They stopped and Henry looked down. Three vultures fed and did not move from their feast of corpse. He identified what was left as a horse, a wild mustang most likely and he looked across the field at the hundreds more. It was not the work of Comanche and if word had reached Parker there would most certainly be hell to pay and tenfold.

He knew Parker and not just of him. He had met this half breed on several occasions. He first heard of him as a fierce and deadly warrior in the lands of Texas in which tales of his fighting bravery were of myth and legend. He could not be matched in the savagery of battle. He was never beaten and never caught.

Later Henry would meet him as a business acquaintance with savvy and honesty. It was hard to put the two together. Parker was an enigma, a chameleon of sorts, highly intelligent and slightly insane.

But Henry had no issues with Parker and preferred to keep it that way. He knew him as a man of his word and that was not always a good thing.

I can't believe you'd prefer to stand here in the middle of this, Jed said. Yer stupidity is quickly becoming a concern, Henry.

"Stupidity, where'd you ever hear a word like that?"

Zee, says it. I feel eyes on us now, stupid.

"Zee does? Say it again, so I can get it right."

Stupidly.

"Who's she say that about? Never mind. The man to worry about would not judge me for this."

What about the man back in that town?

"Shut up now, trying to think."

Well' ya know what they say?

"No, what do they say?"

More folks die in the first week of the month than the last.

"What the hell's that got to do with it?"

I don't know.

"That's stupidity. The stupidest thing I ever heard."

You know what the stupidest thing I ever heard?
"No, and I don't want to, so shut the hell up."
Yer gonna get us killed.
"Shut up now, I'm thinkin."
Killed.
"Stop."

Although Parker had put his war aside years ago and did what no other Comanche had done, adapt to the whites and exploit their treaties for his own gain and self-preservation. He lived now and remained a capable and powerful man in a different way. A judge without mercy, a shrewd cattleman, horse trader and would not take to the murder of horses. His response would be capitol, just and swift. He was one of the few men that's very presence could make Henry uneasy. Henry knew Jed was right and best to make distance from this killing field.

They left it behind for the high plains and once Henry felt they were far enough he decided to make camp near a creek that ran hidden and lonely in the grass of a wide open meadow. The sheltering forest walls were far away and all around and looked like black serrated blade there against the starry sky.

He unsaddled Jed and gathered what wood he could find and made a fire and a comfortable camp.

Still he sat unsettled. He cursed himself while he re-saddled Jed and kept his rifle near. The sounds of the bubbling creek would drown out the sound of approaching dangers and he cursed himself for this too but stayed there anyway. He was tired.

Zee had sent a little coffee and a tin to brew in. Henry drank and smoked the cigar he got from the bank. Bittersweet it was and sleep over took him as soon as he laid his head.

Sleeping lightly and of a dream both bizarre and clear, he turned over and over. He saw an army the likes of which were not of the waking world. Men of different clothes, mixed uniforms and hats of all sorts and they traveled hard and fast and left all in their wake in flames and death and it burned behind them like a great wave of destruction.

Not even in the war and in his own conduct during had he seen such leveling by a given force.

They rode horses gargantuan and rabid with blood lust. Heads rolled and lobbed against their sides, mummified faces locked in horror, Indians, women, children. The coats of Hell's Army were made of scalps and flapped in the wind. Their leader carried a long staff shaped like a cross of the Christian with a bloodied point on the top raised to the sky. The others were outfitted with long rifles and pistols of all shapes and sizes, makes and models. The ground roared and trembled for miles before them like the end of a world, and it was.

Henry had heard of such an army long in the past and in the lands of old Mexico but had always doubted their truth and delivery. He watched under his closed lids with wonder and interest.

Jed woke him with a kind of a scream that Henry had never heard from him before and he sat up and shook the dream away. Jed galloped in a circle, dug his hoof at the earth and jerked his head violently around. They're comin for us Henry. I told you.

Henry stood and looked to the east. A wall of dust covered the rising sun far away. He couldn't hear over the creek. "Probably just a dust storm," he told Jed. "Calm down."

But Jed persisted in his tirade, remembering the field of dead kin. Storms come from the west, stupid.

"I know that."

Then let's believe it Henry. Let's believe that and act like we know it.

Zee woke within the same sunrise and commenced cooking a breakfast of bacon and flap jacks and sat at the table and just looked at it all. She drank a cup of coffee and took one bite of bacon. It was salty and disagreed and she put the rest back on the plate and brushed her hands on her apron. She stood, walked over and took the shotgun from the safe and set it near the bolted door. She didn't know why but something had led her to do it.

She wandered through the house dusting and straightened things that didn't need dusting or straightening. She walked from room to room and stood or sat in each one for a bit of time and eventually made her way outside. She fed what cattle they had left and cleaned Jed's stall. The old mare they used for the wagon and Jed's company stood in her place, chewed oats and watched her activities with curiosity.

Completing the chores she left the barn and walked out to the wood pile and spilt a few logs with an axe that was there, dull and heavy with rust. She began to make a list of chores in her mind for Henry beginning with having that axe sharpened.

She kept chopping wood until she was out of breath and sweat pasted her hair to the sides of her face and the back of her neck. She placed what she could carry in her cradling arms and stacked it neatly against the house on the porch, safe from the rain.

A chicken had taken interest in her doing Henry's work and walked in front of her picking the ground and zigzagging between her feet. She nearly tripped twice before she returned to the log pile and rested her arm on the axe handle. She watched this chicken with its beady eyes and wretched beak. Something from child hood had made her suspicious of chickens. She thought them evil, even as she ate them.

She reached down and grabbed it by the spurs, slammed it on the cutting stump, gripped the axe up high and dropped it on its neck. She tossed it off in the yard and watched it run in a circle spraying blood in an interesting pattern in the dirt until it dropped over and laid still.

A rider alone on the horizon and some distance away was approaching. She watched for a while and went back in the house and stood by the door and waited.

Henry had no time to break camp but most of his provisions were on Jed. They leapt through the creek and headed for the forest that was maybe three or five miles away. They rode fast and hard still not knowing the company behind or their reasons for being. He didn't suspect they were friendly and Jed had been acting strange since Independence. He thought it best they stay in the same mind.

He looked over his shoulder several times hoping the dust would settle and turn away but it stayed fast and only grew. The forest was coming closer in view to where he could now make out the species of trees that lived there. Jed ran sure footed and with all he had as saliva sprayed from his mouth and snot from his nose. The wind bellowed in their ears. Henry laid his head next to Jed's neck for a lower profile and let him go where he wanted.

The timber came up fast and Jed tore through the first of the trees as Henry pulled back on the reins. The horse fought the stop but eventually came to a skidding halt and Henry turned him around. They walked back to the tree line and looked out.

Ya think their Indians? Jed said.

"No, I don't."

I don't like what you got us into.

"I don't like it much either."

How bout, you wait here and see what they want, offer em some jerk, and I'll just go on and wait for ya?

"How about you shut it up?"

Its good plan, best I can think of.

Henry let out a deep sigh and watched.

The sun was up and the dust had stopped moving but lingered in place. They were at the camp. Jed reared up and nearly threw Henry to the ground. He lost the reins and grabbed the saddle horn and tried to retrieve them as Jed jerked, kicked and circled. Henry dismounted quickly, grabbed him by the bit and said, "Stop, stop it goddamn it. What's wrong with ya?"

Jed snorted but relaxed a little and said, we have to go; every dawn has its day.

Henry looked out across the horizon. The dust had commenced again and was growing. "Alright," Henry said. "But it's every *dog*, every *dog*."

That makes no sense. What would a dog do with a day?

"Sleep I spect."

I don't like dogs.

"Yeah I know. It don't goddamn matter none though."

He grabbed the reins and climbed up and Jed ran through the timber with reckless desperation.

Henry headed south and circle behind them. If they had good trackers and Henry knew they did, going home was not yet an option. He had to lead them away up into the rocks where tracking was hard and a position for fighting was at his advantage. They would think he was heading for Texas and then Mexico. He needed to find or create an opportunity to vanish.

The timber was the only thing that sheltered them from view and soon that became lean and gone altogether and opened up to a country of low grass field and rolling hills. A small farm off to the south held little interest for either Henry or Jed, and except for one pig, a few dogs barking at the sky and a small boy walking about, it looked abandoned and let gone the way side.

Henry pushed Jed and made for the red rock ridge a few miles over. He didn't look back for this was open territory and if a bullet from long rifle had his name on it, so be it.

Jed struggled through the loose rock at the base of the little mountains and they made their way into a narrow canyon. It was a pass, well-traveled and with high rocks on both sides. It reeked of danger and they moved fast through and up to a flat iron and into a crevice at the opening of a large cave. Henry stepped down. Jed spoke his disapproval of the situation again but allowed himself to be tied off to a dead Cyprus stump that had been born and died in an unfortunate place.

Think I could get some water Henry? Just a drink before we die?

"Oh for Christ sake," Henry said and took his canteen pushing Jed's head up and poured the water in the side of his mouth. He took a swallow himself, tied it back to the saddle horn and slid the rifle from its scabbard and began to climb. It was hard going. He was just fifty, past middle age for these times though and he had to rest twice before he reached the summit.

What do ya see? Jed said.

The world grew large in a wide angle at the top and he laid down flat with his rifle beside him and looked out. He could see the party coming across the plain. They had shrunk in size to about ten men. He didn't have to wonder why. They were smart and knew.

Henry thought about Zee alone at the ranch. He could see the cross timbers behind them. He could see the old farm there, a mud patch and shack in the golden earth. He pulled a spy glass from his breast pocket, a spoil from a union captain he'd killed years ago. He steadied on his elbows and focused. Two of the men were not clothed in the usually manner for a posse. They dressed well, clean shaven and their white shirts glowed like uniforms behind black string ties. They wore the hats and clothes of pilgrims but their boots and arms were that of killers. The rest looked to be farmers and merchants and ill equipped for long distant riding.

What do ya see?

Henry lowered the glass and bit his bottom lip and watched as they approached the farm and one by one they spread out and circled it. One talked to the boy and his pig from his saddle. He gave himself up as the leader and first on Henry's kill list. Henry put the glass back to his eye and focused again. The man had a hard face, deep eye sockets, and a long mustache, waxed and black. The boy was listening and shaking his head no when the man drew a large caliber pistol. The puff of blood left the back of the boys head before the sound of the shot reached Henry ears. Henry lowered the glass and furrowed his brow. A woman came shrieking from the cabin to the boy. Some words were passed before she pointed toward the rocks and Henry. They looked before shooting her dead as well.

Jed heard the shot as well and said, shit, Henry, what going on out there?

Henry watched as they killed the pig, two dogs and set the little kindled shack to blaze. They scalped the boy and woman and tied the hair to their saddles, making it look like the work of Indians and left the bodies there in the dirt.

They regained a loose formation and rode hard and fast toward the pass where Henry had entered.

"Alright then ya sons a bitches, if that's the way it's gonna be."

Henry stood up and walked over to a tree limb lying nearby. He pulled his pistols and placed them on the flat rock there. He leaned his rifle against the limb and removed his ammunition belt and laid it out flat. He spied their progress and took what was left of the cigar, lit it, lay on his back and puffed hard, blowing the smoke skyward for them to see. He picked up the rifle and weighed it his hands and got comfortable with the barrel resting across the log.

If they had seen the smoke they made no signs of it. They kept a hurried pace and came on into Henry's range.

Henry let out a deep breath and set the cigar aside. He checked the wind. There was none. He looked at the sun straight over head. A flock a pheasant skidded across the prairie floor behind the men riding. He nested the rifle against his shoulder and adjusted his sights. He could now hear the drum of their hooves. He steadied the bead just ahead and above the chest on the man with the mustache and drew a deep breath and squeezed the trigger. The man flew backward off his horse, and was drug there for a while till his boot came off and there he stayed. The horse and other men kept riding as if nothing had happened.

Henry looked on with curiosity.

He breeched another cartridge and dropped another with a shot to the head that burst like a melon. That one stayed up right for a while. His headless body bounced in the saddle before sliding off to the side and to the ground. He reloaded again and another fell and they began to split up and they rode hard and fast and soon they were in the shelter of the rocks. Henry gathered his arms and slid down the trail to where Jed was waiting.

You sure got yourself in a pickle, Henry.

Henry looked at Jed. "Yer in it with me."

If I get killed, I won't forgive you.

"I wouldn't blame ya none."

He mounted and led Jed back up the canyon straight toward the advancing company. There was a bend in the trail that he remembered just before where the rocks were close together and the path was only wide enough for one rider at a time. There and just out of sight he pulled back on the reins, tied them to the horn and pulled his pistols. Jed danced and circled. His adrenaline pumped like fuel for an engine of war. Henry gripped the horse with his knees and waited calm and patient.

Jed said, end this, Henry.

The sound of hoof beats echoed through the canyon and grew louder with each passing second. They advanced without caution or care and the first man came between the rocks and Henry shot him dead.

Then the second and third, then rifle shots from somewhere off, great and many blended with the sounds of Henry's working colts and Jed's snorts of defiance. He killed two more and then no more were coming and his guns were hot and smoking. He holstered them and drew the rifle, waited and watched the opening as the men's horses kicked about in the dust, confused and lost.

Silence fell as the horses all ran off their own way and Henry took Jed a few steps closer to the bend, shouldered the rifle and looked through. More dead men lie in the trail and on the rocks were their mounts had left them and nothing moved.

Jed stepped carefully through twisted bodies and they passed through the rocks and stood in the trail. Henry looked up.

Indians.

Comanche, high in the hills and on both sides held their rifles on him, too many to kill and nowhere to run, for Henry knew that they had also positioned themselves at his back as well. He lowered his gun and waited for their purpose.

Yer fucked, Jed said.

Henry drew a deep breath and whispered, "fuck you."

They'll like me. I'm a good horse. You, not so much.

"If they'd wanted me dead, I'd be dead by now."

Look what's comin. Look at that.

Up the trail a figure appeared on a painted pony dressed for war and running toward them at full gallop. Henry strained to see. The Indians face was covered red, with the eye sockets black and in a crazed grimace he came at them with intimidation, but Henry held Jed in his tracks.

He wore a Union Jacket over a bare back and three eagle feathers braided in the side of his hair. He brought his paint to a skidding halt in front of them and screamed as he drew his knife from his buckskin boot and slashed at the air close and around them. He circled Henry and Jed and tested their fear. Henry looked in the warriors eyes and in there he saw nothing of patience, kindness or mercy. And he knew the man for what he was and the importance of the moment.

Bird spoke in Comanche and Henry knew little of the language but could not mistake the tone and delivery. He shook his head, no. Bird snarled his face and gritted his teeth like the very taste of English was poison on his lips. "You will come."

"I cannot do that," Henry said.

The man bulged his eyes as if anger was to overtake him and the Indians in the rocks cocked their rifles and drew down upon them. This time the young man screamed it. "You will."

Henry swallowed hard and stared the man down.

The brave road off up the trail and did not look back. Henry looked at the bodies on the floor of the trail and the men in the hills with their rifles and faces of death.

Please don't do anything stupid, Henry. I think we should at least see what they want, Jed said.

"Yeah, maybe so."

They rode out of the canyon at a fast pace and onto the prairie. They passed through the farm where the hairless bodies of mother and child lay bloody and staring up in the mid-day sun while all they ever owned burned around them.

The young man circled his horse around the bodies and looked at them with great intensity. He looked a Henry and scowled, knowing he had brought this senselessness with him and Henry saw that the man did not approve of him. The red face did not agree with his company or his assignment.

He shouted at Henry in his native tongue and waved his hand over the scene. Henry adjusted himself in the saddle. "Let me be, and I'll kill em."

The Indian shook his head. "I have already killed them. If it were up to me, you would be dead too."

"There are more."

"Yes," he said. "Always more," and he kicked his horse and they continued on. Henry looked back at the black smoke circling into the sky.

Zee stood in the doorway as the rider approached and stopped near the barn. "Mrs. Faro," he called out.

She didn't reply but narrowed her eyes and picked up the gun and held it in view.

"Mrs. Faro, it's Jake Olson. Sheriff Olson. I'm a friend.

"I know the names of my friends," She called back. "I don't know yours."

"A friend a yer husband, a friend a Henry's. We's in the war together." He made a gesture with his hands that Zee had recognized, one she saw her husband make before in greetings with other ex-confederates, Knights of the Golden Circle, but it did not hold the trust it once did.

"You'n about a million others."

He looked down at the dead chicken and spit. He looked back and walked the horse a few steps closer. Zee pulled the hammers back on both barrels and placed the butt against her shoulder.

He stopped knowing he'd only get peppered from that distance, but still. "Henry home?"

"He's huntin, and close by too. Just stay where ya are. I can hear ya fine."

"I don't mean no harm to ya mam. I'll stay here, just wanted a word with, Henry."

"Well, I told ya, not here, but he's close by and he's a good shot from there too."

The man removed his hat and pulled his handkerchief and patted his brow. He looked around and across the plains to the low mountains and back at Zee.

"Yes mam, I know that's true. Listen up, got a telegraph from Kansas about an hour ago."

"Good for you."

"Would ya lower the weapon please, Mrs. Faro. I'm not here for that."

"Nother, good for you."

"Just tell him when ya see him some folks up in Independence say they'd seen him that way, callin him by his old name."

She felt her chest heave and tears well up and she fought them off. "My husband ain't got but one name, and he sure as hell ain't got no business with Jayhawkers."

"Just lettin him know. I know the Sheriff up there. Henry knows him too. He's a man to think about, serious like. And you should take an interest in this information."

"Well, ya let us know, now get gone."

He pursed his lips and leaned against the saddle horn for a moment. He brought his fingers to the brim and gave a quick nod. He untied a burlap sack from the saddle with whisky, flour and candy and let it drop to the ground. "Good day then Mrs. Faro, pleasure."

He turned the horse around and rode away. Zee stood and watched. He looked back at her a couple a times before he broke into a full stride and shimmered away in the heat.

Henry was led south by the party. He was not in capture for they made no attempt to disarm him. And the braves rode at a distance all around and occasionally they would take turns riding up close and inspecting him with contempt and then ride back out, hollering war cries and watching.

He knew the Comanche word for bird and had figured by eave dropping that that was the young brave's name who led this party.

Bird stayed a hundred yards ahead of Henry as they rode and if that distance was threatened a brave would ride up, cross between them and slow Jed back.

Bird did not look back. His shoulders were broad and his posture was strong. He held his rifle up away from his horse and did not tire from its weight. He was an impressive figure and Henry dreaded the thought of killing him.

Late in the day they came upon the killing fields of wild horses and Bird finally turned on his horse and looked at Henry with more disapproval and blame. He stepped his horse slowly through the massacre and looked at each one. The stench did not seem to bother him and Henry fought to contain the same composure. Jed was not as unaffected and pulled hard to get through it all.

It was in this late light of day that Henry noticed a brand on the haunch of one of the rotting carcasses and he knew it. It was a star shaped brand, the brand of Parker. The same brand Bird's little paint carried. Henry did not feel good about it and wished he hadn't noticed it all. At this time he had also noticed Bird's size, stature and over all resemblance to Parker.

They turned south and rode hard and fast across open territory as the crow flies and there was nothing on the horizon to look forward to, no timber, no mountains, or shelter of any kind. And the sky in the west seemed to churn and pulse. They all tried to ignore its looming presence but none could resist looking from time to time.

As they rode on silently into the lower plains the day passed into evening and the grass became thin and the soil was hard and worthless. Small black blotches of buffalo off in the distance lingered and grazed, gaunt and mangy. Henry looked out at the animals he thought to be extinct. He knew they were nearing reservation land, for only that land could inhabit such a lack of value.

Wild mustangs in the hundreds looked on and played and ran in their herds and among themselves like children on a toy-less playground. The only color and beauty that existed in this world was theirs and in the sunsets, unknowing and un-deliberate. Jed watched them from time to time and they conversed telepathically in their own wild way

Reverend Poole led his posse of Christians across the high plains of no man's land. He knew the man Henry Faro by his given name. He did not share this knowledge with the assembly for they knew of the man that Henry was and all believed that that man had been killed many years ago.

Suspicion and fear was the Reverends tools and his to hold. He would not allow rumors of the walking dead to sway their faith in him. The thought itself made him uneasy.

They had taken separate roads in the war, Poole, a captain under McClelland at a time when Henry had taken up with Quantrill. Poole knew first hand Henry's capabilities.

Quantrill and his raiders had taken war to another level, one that Poole agreed with but for different reasons. But they would not have this preacher type in their likes, for Poole could not follow and was considered a fanatic and unhinged and eventually relieved of duty with dishonor.

Quantrill kept a well-oiled machine of many parts that worked together with precision, trust and honor for the south. God had no place in it.

Quantrill raiders had no room for the distractions of religion that Poole carried with him like weapons. Religion in war was like a heavy blanket on a hot day.

The Reverend could still taste the bitterness of rejection on his tongue. He leaned over, spit and a silent revenge that was not of the bank robbery returned from memories far away and nights long ago, and it grew and drove him on as his riders swept through the land from farm to ranch and they relieved all from their sin and left behind a swath of death, fire and ash.

The deputy, William Rhoar, rode up next to him and shouted. "He didn't come this way, Reverend. There's no tracks to see of."

Poole glared at William. "He will. The devil will returnith from which he was spawned and I'll be waiting and I will slay him where he sleeps. His whore awaits him. It was given to me in a vision."

William studied Poole's face and felt fear deep inside, fear of wrong doing. He was a hired man and had never given in to what Poole was selling but he had never questioned the hand that fed either.

This was different though. He looked up ahead into the setting sun, bleeding across the horizon and turned his mount back to the flank of the party. William fell in next to another and they shared gazes and he shook his head. "I don't like it. Don't like it much at all."

"The Reverend will deliver us," the rider said and looked straight ahead.

Soon in the distance a structure appeared ahead of them. Henry watched as it grew with their arrival. The home of Parker, a large estate of wood and many gables with white inverted stars painted on its roof. Figures scurried about, women, children, horses, men and other livestock. The other braves rode on up ahead and took their places in the compound. Bird rode to the far end of the porch, turned his horse, stopped and watched Henry walk Jed to the front steps. Jed looked around, confused, tired and thirsty but said nothing.

An old man sat on a stool, throwing a knife into the wood floor repeatedly in a game of mumble peg as he argued aggressively with himself and the floor. Henry knew the man, Missouri, a life before, but did not greet him. He watched and waited.

A young squaw emerged from the front door, followed by another and then another, and they kept coming and they lined up against the house with their faces down and equaled five.

The old man on the stool took interest and worked his brows toward Henry and his eyes widened. "I'll be damned'n the riva's gonna rise," he said. "That really you boss?"

"Hello Charlie," Henry said.

Charlie leaped off his stool and ran to a porch post nearest to Henry and wrapped his arms around it as if the earth was turning too fast for standing. "It's you. Ho-ly shit."

"Henry, Faro." A deep voice growled from the darkness of the open door and Parker stepped out and grinned. His form enormous, his head double the size of a normal man and he stepped forward in a black wool three piece suit, speckled with dust and lint. His hair in braids lay down the lapels. He carried a cane that he did not need for walking and stood next to Charlie. His eyes as black and polished onyx shifted from Henry to Charlie who still stood clinging to the post slack jawed in disbelief.

He smacked Charlie across the back of his head with the cane and Charlie slid down the post to his knees and began shinning Parker's shoes with spit and sleeve.

Parker smiled at Henry. "It is good to see again, Henry Faro. How good of you to visit."

"Not like I had much of a choice," Henry said and nodded to Bird still mounted and glaring at Henry.

Parker looked over. "Bird, my oldest son."

"Bird," Henry said and nodded the young man.

"George Washington Parker. But he does not like that name."

Bird spit on the ground and Parker laughed. "He is not pleased with it. But that is his name." His mother calls him, Bird. It agrees with him better, and so he is, Bird.

Henry watched Charlie crawl after Parker as he walked across the porch close to Henry. Charlie picked the lint from Parker's pant leg and muttered to himself.

"Why did ya have me brought here, Parker? My destination is of great urgency and this delay could cost me."

He looked at the Red Face Bird and back at Henry. "Did you know the president of the United States visited me, just a week past?"

"I did not."

"Yes, we hunted wolves together. We are best friends now."

"That's wonderful, Parker." Henry began to protest more but Parker raised a giant hand to stop him.

"Your recent activities came to me in a dream, Henry, and spoken to me by a hawk that saw. I sent Bird to help you pass. I must say; your lack of gratitude is surprising."

"I didn't ask for your help."

"But you needed it regardless. You would be dead now if I had not."

"I've been dead before. It's not as bad as folks make out."

"Agreed, Faro." Parker laughed, smiled and looked down at Charlie still shinning his shoes and kicked the old man away. He scurried back to his stool and sat staring at Henry muttering incoherently and shaking his head.

Parker pulled a gold watch from his vest and checked the time and looked at the sky for confirmation. "You will join me for dinner and we will break bread together like old friends do."

"I reckon not," Henry said.

"Yes, you will," said Parker and turned back toward the door. "Then we will discuss your debt."

Henry let out a deep sigh and watched Parker slide back into the darkness of the door. His wives followed one by one, obediently and single file. Charlie sat on his stool, swatted at Parker's air and scratched and picked at himself, muttering and stuttering. "Sons a bitch."

Bird charged his horse up next to Henry and pulled Jed's reigns from his hands.

Jed tried to jerk them back but Bird was strong and intimidating. He looked at Henry and said, "go," and nodded toward the door.

Henry took a quick count of the men nearest to him. More had gathered since their arrival. He swung his leg across Jed's back and dismounted and walked around pulling the reins from Bird's hands. He tied Jed to the porch post and stepped up to the door. Henry glanced down at Charlie, muttering still and arguing with what was left of his sane self and went inside.

The parlor was dark with shadows from the simple wood work that decorated the walls and ceiling. The floor was dirty and planked like a barn in contradicting craftsmanship.

Henry walked through and into the dining room and lifted off his hat. Parker sat at the head of a long and sturdy table and the women stood and waited behind their chairs. Oil lamps lined the walls and lit the room with a dim sense of motion. Henry stepped up to the empty chair at the far end and a pig squealed from under the table and ran for the darkness of a hall.

Parker waved his hand at Henry's place at the table. "The President of the United States of America sat there."

Henry pulled the chair out and sat. His weaponry under his coat was now uncomfortable. He pulled his knife from the back of his belt and laid it on the table.

"We hunt together." Parker said. "We are great friends."

Henry studied Parker and said, "So I heard. It's very important that I get back, Parker. Time is short."

Parker put a finger to his bottom lip and looked at Henry a long time. "Yes, it is," he said and removed his finger and picked up a folded napkin. The the women, all but the two at his sides, began to sit in several awkward ways, all as if trying something new and not getting it right.

"You know," Parker said. "They told me I could have but one wife here and that I must choose and tell the rest to go. Do you know what I told them, Henry?"

Henry bit his bottom lip and adjusted himself more comfortably and placed his arms on the table. "No, I do not."

Parker looked at his wives and smiled. "I told them; tell them yourself." And his giant face broke into laughter and his eyes bulged, sparkled and gleamed. And then he stopped at once and turned stoned face and serious.

"Is there something you wanted from me, Parker? I must be going. I don't mean no disrespect but as we pass time here..."

"I understand," Parker said as the two of the wives filled his plate and cut his meat. "The man who you worry about is diseased. He is crazy with his white God who excuses all he does. I've heard many men that travel through his town are never seen again. He has cost me much in horses as I think you have seen. And the dead he leaves behind are scalped, raped, and I think you know who gets blamed for that."

"Do you know this man, Parker?"

"I do not, but word has traveled far of his power and conviction. His weapons are in his words and they say he can make the rain with them. What do you think of that, Henry?"

Parker spread his arms and the two women standing finally sat unfed in chairs on either side of him. He began picking at his food with his fingers and chewing his meat and looking at Henry.

"I reckon I don't believe a man can do that."

"They say he gets these powers from the bible. They call him, a Rain King."

"Sounds like they say a lot."

Parker stopped chewing and looked at Henry curiously. "You do not believe these things I'm saying?"

Henry thought about it for a while and he thought about Zee and all her reading and prayers and reciting of passages and he reflected quickly on his life's images and memories. "I don't believe no man can make it rain."

Parker leaned back in his chair and commenced chewing. "That's interesting, Henry."

"Why is that so interesting?"

"Well, I have seen many things and I have made many voyages out of this body." Parker paused, swallowed and studied the table cloth. "I think if a man believes something strong enough, he can make it so."

"I've been trying hard to believe that I'm not your prisoner. Is that so?"

Parker looked at Henry with astonishment. "Prisoner? We are friends, are we not, Henry Faro?"

"I always thought so."

"Then it is so. Eat, eat." Parker nodded to the food across the table.

Henry sat back in his chair. "Parker, why did you bring me here? Why don't you just tell me what you want? If you know the things you say, then you know I must go."

Parker straightened his back and continued chewing, staring at Henry as if he were a painting on the wall. When he finished and swallowed he took a deep breath, let it out and rolled his eyes around the ceiling. "They say this man charms the snakes too." He stopped and shook his head tight and pointed a greasy finger at Henry. "He speaks with the snakes, Henry. Now that is evil."

Parker picked out a potato from his plate and held it up before him and looked at Henry. "I want you to kill this man, Henry. I want you to kill, this Rain King."

Henry's eyes shifted from Parker and along the rows of wives who sat silent with their hands in their lap and their eyes upon their empty plates. "I have no reason, Parker."

Parker nodded in agreement and shrugged. "You had no reason to steal his money either, but that didn't stop you." He raised his eyebrows and nodded his head. "How much money did you take from him?"

Henry pursed his lips and studied Parkers face in search of the intentions of his question. "Enough, more than enough to start a new life and that's what I intend to do. That's all intended to do."

Parker belched and put a napkin to his lips and waited, and then he smiled. "You can a buy a life? Where do they sell those? You can start a new life by applying the tools of an old one? That sounds foolish to me. And yet killing for men like you is as natural as breathing and you say you need a reason. I do not understand the white ways, but I've become very good at pretending to. It is amusing to see you whites scurry about with your reasons for this and that, buying lives." Parker shook his head, amused.

"I don't care what you do or don't understand, Parker. I set out to do what I did and that's the end of it. I have nothing against this man or his town. I have no reason to want him dead."

"Something in the wind has told me differently, that there is more. But never mind that. I do not understand everything, but I understand more of the white's every day and it is why I brought you here. You say that is the end of it. There is no end to it. You people always say, 'that's the end of it,' when there is no end to any of this. There is no end to a circle Henry. It keeps going and going and going. You understand? It is nothing and yet it is all"

"I understand you, Parker, but we all have reasons for the things we do, even you."

"Very well, Henry. You need reasons? You shall have them. Now when the sun has crossed the sky twice from this night you will have them." Parker shoved a potato whole into his mouth and chewed smiling. "Right?"

Henry thought about that while Parker ate and swallowed. "Why don't you just kill him yourself?"

"No, I cannot. I am retired from that life. I'm a statesman now, Henry, a judge. I have a friend in the President. My days of that are over. You, you are a killer, Henry. That's what you are, what you have. Like a bird has wings, it flies. That is what it is does. It is expected of you to behave as such."

"I am retired from that life too Parker."

Parker smiled. "If that were true, we would not be meeting this way."

Henry wondered how Parker knew but not enough to ask. It was unimportant in the scheme of things. Besides, Parker's explanations, if he felt like giving any, would be confusing and shrouded in metaphors. The boy, Bird and his riders had not come upon him by accident; In fact it was clear now that they had been sent. Parker was a smart and strategic man in every sense and he had spies everywhere.

"And this deed you ask of me, Parker, what's in it for me."

Parker dropped his hands with a boom and the unused table wears shook and rattled. "I am not asking, Henry. I'm growing fat and tired with this food and this conversation." He pushed his plate and setting to the floor. "Besides, you are dead already. And that has been a secret to all but a few up until now. Now that secret has been broken and it will be known if it is not laid back to rest. You will be hunted again, and you will be caught. That is what's in it for you. There is your reason. And if that is not enough, go home, and you will see. If you dare, you will find another. You need to spill blood as badly as you need the air and you know it."

Henry bit his lip and worried Parker's words were true. He had painted himself into a fine corner. Hasty activities often produce such results and Henry's mind was working for a way to right it. He had been reckless all his life but luck favors the youth and eventually they both run out together.

"Who is this man to you, Parker?"

Parker had nodded off or pretended to but looked up from the table at Henry. "Don't pretend you don't know. You know him and he knows you."

Memories of the past filled his mind's eye once again. "Never heard of him," he lied.

Parker cocked his head and waited before he smiled and spoke. "That is smart, Henry, not to acknowledge the dead. It is bad luck to speak the enemy's name.

Henry stood up with a nod to Parker and his wives and pushed the chair up to the long restless table. He lifted his hat. "We'll meet again, Parker."

"Yes we will, Henry Faro. But only as sprits I think. We will both cross the great river soon."

Henry walked across the floor to the doorway and Parker called out, "Henry, you didn't eat. Was it not a good meal?" The wives eyes darted to one another and they all fidgeted for a good answer.

"Dead men don't eat, Parker," he said and walked down the dark hall toward the door.

Henry heard his laughter echo through the large house as he stepped out onto to the porch in the cool of the night.

Charlie was waiting in the dark and sprang at his leg, "Take me with ya old friend, ya can't imagine this place, ya can't. Parker ain't... Parker ain't right. He ain't right in the head. I could tell ya stories friend that'd make yer hair curl. All his spooky injun magic shit. We go back, we got history you and me. Take me, please boss."

"I'm sorry Charlie but I'm not headed nowhere any better."

"I don't care. Hell itself'd be better'n here. Take me."

Henry looked at Charlie and stepped off the porch. He untied Jed and felt the leather reigns slip through his hands and said. "Take us to the well, Charlie."

"It's right over yonder boss, just follow me. You'll see, I can still be a help."

They walked across the ranch to the corrals. Indians stood all around in the moonlight and watched like totems or sleeping cattle as they reached the stone circle with its tiny shed roof.

"It'll be just like the old days, ride'n and shoot'n," Charlie said as he lowered the bucket down. "We'll make so much goddamn money we can't carry it all."

"Sure thing Charlie, just like the old days," Henry said and pulled his half smoked cigar from his breast pocket.

"We'll get the whole gang back together, you'll see." Charlie cranked the handle and brought the water bucket up and fought it onto the stone ledge.

Henry struck a matched and puffed and smiled at Charlie and Charlie smiled back. "The whole gang is dead Charlie. All dead."

Charlie's smile went away but he kept optimistic. "We'll that's alright. We'll get a new gang, a better'n, you'll see."

Charlie let the bucket drop to the ground for Jed and the water soaked Henry's boot and darkened there. He could feel the cold seeping through. Henry pulled his cigar from his lips and looked down at it. "Ah hell, Charlie."

Charlie huffed and tried a smile, wiping Henry's boot with his dirty fingers. He looked up at Henry. "I'm real sorry bout that boss."

"Me too, Charlie."

Henry's eye's flickered in the moonlight as he drew a deep breath and looked about the ranch.

He thought a favor for an old friend was in order. He pulled his cold Colt from its holster and placed the barrel to Charlie's forehead and pulled the trigger. The shot cracked the air of the night. There was no echo back and it was gone in an instant. Charlie Dropped over and was through.

Jed raised his head from the bucket and looked at Charlie and then at Henry and said, I was hoping you'd do that, and went back to drinking.

Henry looked over the compound and through the standing Indians back to the porch of the ranch. Parker stood under the eve in the dark there watching. He smiled, nodded his head in approval, slid his hands in his pockets, turned and went back inside.

Zee had spent the afternoon doing the chores but the words of the morning visitor followed her around like a swarm of flies.

The sack he brought lay where he left it. She sat on a stump in the evening as the sun fell but it had lost its beauty and she didn't notice.

She kept her gaze to the east and minutes turned to hours before she realized she was being consumed and crippled by worry. She stood and pulled the axe from the stump where it was lodged and heaved it toward the house but it fell only a few feet from where she stood.

"Damn you." She shouted and cursed herself more so than anyone else.

She kicked a chicken and feathers puffed about but it only hopped off as she marched past to the house and to the pantry.

She drug a steamer trunk through the door, banging and scratching the sides as she labored and placed it upright and open in the center of the main living room. Leaping the stairs two at a time she gathered clothes in both arms and threw them over the rail to the floor below.

Franticly she worked gathering shoes and finery she felt needed and important and piled it all in the center of the room downstairs. She stood and looked at it, too much for the trunk and too heavy to carry and she felt overwhelmed with grief and collapsed to her knees and cried into her wedding dress, long yellowed, soiled and worthless.

She sobbed into the silk and rolled in her pride and cried until she could cry no more.

Exhaustion came, caught up with her and pulled her into a deep sleep filled with the dream that Henry had seeded there before he left. Unlike Henry she dreamed in color, she dreamed in scent.

Above her the cattails swayed in a gentle breeze against a tender sapphire sky. She blinked and was fully aware of her reality and the smells of nature filled her, lush and alive.

The water from a river current babbled and spoke in a comforting way and she laid and listened like a hiding child removed from the pains of this world.

This world, was gone, and all greed, deceit, danger, death and treachery were the ingredients of another far away and one of imagination. And she wanted to stay there in this blanket of sundrenched blue and gold forever. She smiled and she closed her eyes as the sun warmed her cheeks.

A perfect scream of a woman clutched in terror, true, elongated, close and it jolted her from this heaven and she opened her eyes and waited. Then another, from a child's throat and she sat up and looked around but the grass was too tall to see.

She rolled onto her knees and with stealth and caution raised herself up and peered out. The sobbing and crying multiplied and drowned out the rushing water as she stood and looked upon a bridge of rusted iron filled with an audience of many who looked down on her with hands and faces in gestures of shock and horror. She waved that she was well and all right but it did not change their reactions.

She stood up and waved both arms and they seemed not see her. They were blinded and swept with emotion. She furrowed her brow and watched them as she stepped to the river's edge and stopped. They were not looking at her but into the water there clear and pristine and they crowded to the rail and some pointed while others clutched and comforted one another.

Zee looked to the water and saw nothing. She leaned down on one knee and placed a hand in its cool current and saw her reflection. She looked into herself, pretty, young, and placed a strand of hair that had fallen behind her ear.

She made a bowl with her hands, closed her eyes and washed her face. The cold on the back of her neck was refreshing in an excellent way and she wanted to share the feeling and to tell them it was good.

She opened her eyes again and her reflection had turned into someone unfamiliar. A man's face, mouth open and with empty eyes just under the surface floating by and rolling away. She wanted to scream like the others but it took her breath and she remembered it was dream.

Standing up she watched it go, bobbing and bloated until it was pulled under and gone.

Letting her eyes drift back up to the sad parade on the bridge she stepped back from the bank and began to walk away and leave them be, but her attention was captured as she turned and noticed out across the water more bodies floating past like tree logs pulled from their roots by a great flood.

Crowded as they were they drifted by as if they belonged, birthed from some great horror upstream and unknown.

She looked upon the gathering on the bridge and recognized some of the clothing and faces as the same as in the water.

She watched and grieved as those lost souls mourned themselves.

"Oh lord," she began but there was not a prayer fitting in her memory for such a sight and she was left faithlessly alone and without words.

Henry rode hard and swift under the cloak of night. The cool air and full stomach had given Jed new wings. They raced across the barren southlands of the reservation and across the prairies and into the high plains. He knew he was being followed and he expected it. He knew it was Bird. What he didn't know he would worry about later. There was time lost and it needed recaptured.

Along with the money for their new life he carried with him Parker's words, Parker's burden. It was a heavy load and it anchored him in his past and complicated things that didn't need complicated.

He thought of the Reverend and the times they shared. He would try all through the night to put those thoughts in the back of mind. He owed Parker nothing he thought and kept telling himself that as if it were true.

But as he passed one burned out farm, and then another and he looked upon the dead stock still in their corrals, the bodies of sharecroppers lying in the ashes and dirt, their bloody limbs hanging from trees and barn beams, good men of hard work and innocence, women and children who had put their faith in Gods who had forgotten them, raped, beaten, scalped, beheaded, skinned alive and then dismembered, he began to change his mind and he slowed his travels as he thought about what he would find at home; the horrors that were his to be.

Night passed to a new day and Bird kept his distance from Henry but stayed with him like a shadow. Henry looked over his shoulder and saw his red face shining in the morning sun like a wild animal bloody from a fresh kill.

When Henry would stop, so would Bird, when Henry rode, so the shadow would follow, pushing him, riding him toward an inevitable place in time that was preordained or destined to be. It had been three days since Henry left home and it felt as if nothing were ever real or even mattered.

With the sun at his back he looked up ahead at the front of a forest, the last forest before entering the panhandle. He thought it a good place to rest Jed and a good place to pull the red faced devil on his back in closer.

There was a small river that fed these trees with high banks and caves. He stopped Jed, tired now and looked back at Bird. Bird slowed to a trot but did not stop, only leaned and crossed his arms on the neck of his paint. It looked as though he whispered something in the horse's ear.

Let them conspire, Henry said to Jed. Let them believe in something of life.

Henry walked Jed into the trees and the wind swayed the high branches above. Fallen limbs crunched under Jed's hoofs upon a bed of leaves that reminded Henry that all things must pass.

But the rush of the creek over the rocks came to them with a promise of at least another day, another hour, another moment of life in this world where everything seemed dead or dying or passing on into something that would not need or want them in its future.

Jed stepped down the bank carefully and into the cold current and began to drink. Are you going to kill him, Henry?

Henry felt the red faced Bird's' eyes upon his back but did not look. "I don't know," he said.

After what he'd seen in the course of the night and what he knew lie ahead, his desire to live was weakening like a rope being stretched to its limits. Jed lifted, turned his head as if to say something of encouragement, hope and self, but Henry's mind was far away.

The world was quietly coming down around them in a heavy promise that an end was near. Bird felt it too, whispers of the other side. He shifted his rifle in his hand.

Henry pulled himself by the horn and swung his leg over Jed's haunches and stood in the stream. He dropped the reins and the horse looked at him with curiosity. He pulled at the fingers of his glove with his teeth, kneeled down and let the water run over his palm and watched his life pass through the clean crystal liquid and over the rocks like a rapid moving dream. It knew all and knew nothing and oh how he wanted to flow with it and be that way too.

He thought and stayed there for a long time just watching the water. Bird stepped his paint in closer, curious and looking.

Henry listened and heard Bird's horse step down the hill. He pulled his pistol from inside his coat, stood and turned and aimed at the boy sitting there at the top of the hill. Bird's back straightened and his red face tightened, and cracked, his horse flinched and he shouldered his rifle. Henry waited and hoped he understood.

Poole entered Sanford that morning in a storm of dust and chaos. They came hard and spread out through this new town bursting with commerce and promise and looked about. There were Indians working next to Chinamen on the Rock Island Railroad. The line had decided to pass Poole's own town and although he thanked the Lord for sparing them the progress his prejudice and jealously raged in quiet place inside. He looked about at the brothels and saloons set up to appease the workers and the cowboys.

Lily laughed, bounced and waved from her window at the men looking up at her. The other girls were more seasoned to the looks of travelers and closed their windows.

There were store fronts filled with color and goods from the east and the west and as far away as Europe. There was a church under construction at the far end of town but had been converted to a lumber stop.

It was Sunday but the town was too busy to notice or care about such things. He spat at the earth below him and bellowed to the skies. "Olson, Jacob Olson. Show yourself and explain this blasphemy."

Shoppers, vender and traders that walked the store front planks retreated to the nearest doors and alleys and watched these strange men, filthy with blood and soot, they looked like corpses that had just left the grave and taken up arms together to ride and kill.

Soon the streets were empty and the only sound was that of a distant steam engine and rhythmic clank of hammers driving spikes in the ever progressive rails. The fact that this world did not, would not stop upon the arrival of God's chosen messenger enraged Poole even more. He showed his teeth and waved his staff and a handful of his troops took flight to inform the workers of their good fortune.

"Olson," he shouted again and the rest of the men spread out down the street and took positions at both ends of the town.

The clank of hammer stopped and the engine in the distance let out a long breath and idled and trembled. Olsen stepped from the door of the cafe and three deputies appeared from other various doorways but stayed in the safety of shade.

"Reverend Poole," Olsen cried out and placed his hands on his pistols and stepped to the street. "You have no jurisdiction here. What do ya want?"

Poole rode hard and fast in Olson's direction and brought his horse to a skidding halt before him. "Where ever the Lord's work is needed, my jurisdiction is seeded. I want the man you call Henry Faro, Olson. Deliver him now and I will bless this, blister of sin you call a town. Deny me and the Lord, and I will burst it like the infected festering boil that is and let it seep back into the hell from which it was birthed."

Olson spat and could feel the men circling around and he looked at Poole. "That's very dramatic Poole, but the Faro's moved on some time ago."

Poole's eyes flickered with lightening. "Lies," Poole seethed. "You lie."

Olsen took a deep breath and sighed. "It's the truth, just up and gone."

William Rhoar rode up next to Poole. He looked at Olsen but spoke to Poole, "He ain't here. That damn witch sent word ahead of us."

Poole straightened his back and turned to Rhoar. "Did I ask for your words? Then keep them." He turned back to Olsen. "Show me where thy devil laid his head and I will leave this town to die the slow and miserable death it deserves."

Olson and Poole were locked in a trance. Olson felt a tear of sweat roll down the side of his face and he wanted to wipe it away but knew any sudden move would not be wise so he stood and suffered. "There's nothin to see, burned the ranch fore he left."

"Liar," Poole screamed. Olsen began to reach for his weapon but was frozen by the sight of Poole's' eyes, the conviction in them and the sounds of other hardware being cocked and readied all around. "Ye have one more chance to give up the man."

Poole's men dragged Lily by her hair from Lucy's saloon into the street, naked kicking and crying. The men, filthy with dust and thoughts ran their hands over her white body while the others held her out. One man stood behind her, cocked his revolver and placed the barrel in the nap of her neck, grinned and showed his rotted gums.

Olsen hesitated and felt the eyes of his people heavy, waiting and he measured the value of each and every one while the steam engine in the near distance huffed and sighed like dragon overcome with sleep. Its breaths came further and further apart, surrendering slowly to the surrounding silence. Even the horses were still and trance like.

The girl twisted and cussed about in the dust of the street.

Olson drew his words up like lifting a great weight and said, "five miles west, Poole. Just follow the road."

William Rhoar let out a deep sigh and shook his head.

Poole grinned and pulled his horse around to face his men and said in an almost whisper. "Send them to Hell. Send them all to Hell."

A gun shot rang out and Lily's pretty face disintegrated in an explosion of blood and smoke before Olsen's eyes and her body fell limp to the ground.

"Nooo!" Olsen cried and drew his pistol only to be cut down in a hail of fire from all directions. Blood flew in the air, bits of flesh and clothes fluttered about as he spun around in the dry street.

Fires had begun in the first of the buildings before he even dropped to his knees.

He fell face first in the street and died, spared of the hours ahead that his town would suffer.

The men rode in all directions; some dismounted and kicked down doors, dragging citizens into the light of day, executing them over their begging, screaming prayers. Children who ran were shot in mid stride, others were allowed to watch as their mothers and sisters were beaten and raped in a horrible orgy of hell on earth before they were killed as well.

The town was ablaze and bodies of the dead lie everywhere. What few attempted escaped were railroad workers who ran horseless and waterless into the emptiness to the east only to be rode down like hunted prey and shot in the back and trampled over by the hoofs of their killers.

And it went on for hours and Poole glowed with delight and rode from one end of the town to the other reciting verse and scripture for the souls of the damned he had taken.

So overcome with the faith in his actions that he felt the presence and approval of his God in his heart and in his mind as his white hair flowed in wind and his face stung from the heat of the burning community and tears poured from his eyes as he outstretched his hands to the sky and thanked the billowing blackened heavens above.

William Rhoar drew the blade of his bowie knife across the throat of an undertaker pulled from his parlor and the last of the screams gave way to the crackling of burning wood, frenzied horses and Poole's sermons ode to the death about.

Rhoar looked at Poole and watched him as he cleaned his blade on the undertakers coat and let him drop to the board walk. There would be no one left to bury this dead.

Rhoar walked to the middle of the street and got on his horse. He pulled his eyes away from Poole and took in his surroundings, the dead, the burning, the carnage, and as he looked up at Poole again his eyes were fixed, mouth clenched in a gleeful grimace, arms open to the sky.

He understood that they had gone too far. They had all gone too far. The promise of salvation for their sins was lost in the passion of its deliverer. He drew his rifle from his saddle and hesitated. Poole pulled his eyes down directly at Rhoar as if being warned and told and Rhoar cowered under his gaze. Poole smiled and put his new knowledge of Rhoar away in a dark pocket and turned his horse and headed west out of town.

The others quickly fell into formation from everywhere and followed. Rhoar spurred his horse and followed as well.

He had promised himself to see the death of Poole and Rhoar did not make promises lightly.

Henry and Bird stood locked in a promise neither wanted to keep. Bird's confusion spread across his red face. Henry held fast and still. He knew that the chance of hitting a man from this distance with a pistol was slim to none and Bird knew it too. He thought about Zee and the kids and the time they shared while the rush of the creek filled his senses like a sweet fragrance, familiar and faint with time.

He thought about what he'd seen in the last few days and what awaited him at the end.

Henry lowered his gun and his head.

Bird lowered his rifle and watched for a moment but could not understand. He had not the intellect of his father. He brought his horse down the hill closer to Henry and watched him there, standing like a man with nothing.

Bird's heart slammed and his veins pulsed. "You are stupid, white man. I know not what father see's. I don't see it. Why would you try to kill me, Henry Faro? I was sent to help you."

Henry didn't look up but said, "If I was trying to kill you... you'd be dead."

"Ha, you are a fool, a fool and a coward."

"Think what you want," Henry said and leaned down toward the water again. His boots filled with chill now and his coat tails drenched were pulled along by the current. He lifted his hat and placed it on the bank and washed his face and neck as Bird thought hard.

Bird did not consider himself a man of deep thought, but a warrior to be, a creature of impulse with one basic instinct and all its applications, the instinct of survival. But he could not help be affected but what they had seen together. The burning towns, the hanging dead, and the hell they chased and would eventually catch up with. He was putting it together now. The strategy of his father's actions in his mind and he felt the position it had put Henry in.

The Comanche had no word for suicide but suddenly Bird felt sheepish and stupid and this angered him even more.

"You want to die, Henry Faro? Then I will kill you. I do not care of some foolish white man. I did not want to come after you. I did not want to come with you. I would just as soon kill you as look at you. You are nothing to me. I am not afraid of you. Can you see that?"

Henry raised his eyes for a moment and looked at the boy. "I see it," he said and went back to washing and drinking.

Jed said, just kill him already.

"I will kill you Henry Faro and feast on your horse, and it will not bother me. You will see."

Kill him now, Henry, Jed said. Just shoot him already.

Bird raised his rifle again at Henry and screamed. Henry ignored him and looked downstream. "Look at me, Henry Faro."

Henry didn't look, but stood, disappointed in Bird and his lack of action over words and turned his back. Parker would have shot Henry for less, cut out his still beating heart and ate it while he watched and died and thought no more of it than he would killing a deer or other game. Bird was not that man.

He pulled Jed's reins from the rushing creek and patted his neck with cool water. He placed his boot in the stirrup and hoisted himself up and into the saddle. He gave Jed a kick and trotted up the other bank. Bird lowered his rifle and watched as Henry went over the hill through the shaded timber.

The sky continued to churn that morning and the winds spoke of the storm that was rapidly approaching.

Henry and Jed walked through the last patch of woods, almost reluctantly. Henry was losing will from exhaustion. Bird followed closer than before but still behind and together they entered the scrub brush and grasslands of the pan handle. Rocks and distant mountains appeared on the far horizon and lay like broken shards of night. Henry bit his bottom lip and watched the grass between Jed's legs as they cut.

Jed was tired and didn't say anything.

Finally Bird couldn't contain himself any longer. The silence from Henry and the long hours riding brought nothing but thought and for young men thought needed expression, confirmation. He understood what had happened at the creek once his anger was rested. "Henry Faro," he said.

Henry did not hear and did not answer but rode on looking at the ground and with each cutting path in the tall grass made by Jed's left hoof. He saw a wound in world that had not been there before.

"Henry Faro," Bird said again and brought his horse up alongside.

Pulling back on the reins Henry stopped and looked at Bird with no expression and asked. "Why do ya wear that death face? There's no more wars, no more battles. They have passed you by. You have lost your war. Your war was lost before it even began."

Bird managed his horse and turned his face from Henry out to the fields. "As long as there is two men standing on the same piece of earth, there will be war, Henry Faro. You know that."

Henry leaned over and spit. He looked at Bird a long time, and then nudged Jed on. Bird stayed alongside this time. "I wanted to tell you, Henry Faro that where we are going is a good a place. It may not look like one, but it is."

"What do ya know bout good places? What do I know? A good place is only in the mind."

Bird rode for a while and thought about that. "Is not war a good place... for warriors?"

"War's just a taste a hell. All it is. A whisper bout where we're headin, and there, will be the rest."

"A taste? And when war is chewed and swallowed, is it not a good feast?"

"No. It's a necessary feast."

"Necessary for life."

"Necessary for men I reckon. It looks that way. Way it's always been."

"It is the circle of life my father says."

"Your fathers a wise man, but he's crazy, got it all wrong."

"It is not the circle of life?"

Henry thought about his own life and path of that life. "More like a square, with hard sharp turns, no right angles, but ya always end up right back to the same place ya started."

"Then let it be so, I say."

Henry thought about what the young man said and nodded. "Yeah, let it be so."

Bird sheathed his rifle for the first time and Henry took note. A red and yellow sky up ahead boiled like a living bruise and a strange silence fell over the world. The smell of rain traveled in from far away and what little life around leaned and begged for its quenching wetness. The sounds of thunder cracked the sky giving way to flashes of lightening within the belly of this great storm. It was going to be a bad one and shelter would be hard to find.

"We are not alike, Henry Faro." Bird finally said and pulled his eyes from the sky. "I do not like your words. I do not agree with them."

"Fine by me, think what ya want."

"You are like all other white men. You kill for gain."

"We all kill for gain, boy. I recon that's the only reason there is."

"No. That is the wrong reason."

Henry stopped Jed and watched the storm swallow up the blue. The wind came now, rich with smells not from this land or of this world.

"You must only kill for sustenance and honor," Bird continued.

Henry turned around and looked behind him at the forest too far away. "Just fancy words for gain. We gotta find shelter soon. I've seen this before. We don't get inside somewhere and neither one of us will ever gain again."

Bird let out a sigh and looked at the sky above and shrugged his face. "There is a cave in those rocks." Bird pointed to the west. "But it is a sacred place we cannot go there. *You*, cannot go there."

"Fuck sacred, it ain't a choice."

They rode hard and fast.

Zee woke from her bed of belongings and gasped and choked until the air filled her lungs. Covered in sweat she rustled to her knees and sat breathing for a long time waiting for the nightmare to weaken. The barn doors outside slammed back and forth like some spirit's tantrum at work. The hinges screeched and screamed. It was dark but not from night. The wind pushed the house with such force it seemed to moan and strained to stay up right.

She could hear the hungry thunder in the clouds rolling overhead, so low it threatened to press her back down as she stood.

She flung an old dress to some far corner and ran to the door. It burst open, pushing her back as she gripped the frame.

The world was swollen, turning and coming in.

She moved to the side of the doorway and pressed herself against the wall and huffed while her many shoes skidded across the floor and dresses danced in the wind like body less puppets on strings. She couldn't hear the livestock. The cows were gone, the chickens too and she knew she too would be swept away if she didn't act fast.

She grabbed a thin garment floating by in the air and wrapped it around the lower half of her face and pulled the shotgun up and pressed it between her breasts. She counted to herself as she struggled out the door. She knew the steps to the barn but had lost count before she left the porch, being pushed back two to one.

The wind wished to lift her off between the house and the barn and she was forced to the ground, crawling and throwing the shot gun along. The dust stung her eyes and blinded her and she fought the scarf up over the rest of her face as she drug herself along.

She could hear a sound that she'd heard before as a child in St Joe and it filled her heart with terror. The sound of a deadly ripping wind bursting her ears and shaking the ground as her body bounced along.

There was funnel near, she knew, coming, dark, hungry and determined to devour.

She had to move. She had to move fast and it took all her strength to gain what ground she could and in her blindness with a sudden walloping pain she was thrust into the air by the barn door and out of the wind where she lay tearing the scarf from her face, coughing, spitting.

She meant to check the ache in her ribs but there was no time for that.

Still blinded, she scratched through the hay on the floor franticly. "Where is it," she screamed. "Where is it? Oh goddamn it please, where is it?"

The twister was on the ranch now and she could hear the splitting of wood and hail, like a thousand arrows against the barn side at once. Light filled her eyelids as the roof of the barn was lifted away and wadded off to some unknown place.

She found the pull ring.

The large brass ring in the floor and she stood and got it up a crack and kick the shotgun down and dropped her feet in.

She let the door rest on her lap while her arms burned and she went for another lift, just enough to lower herself in. The door pushed on her shoulder and scraped the side of her face and came down on her with such gravity that she fell down the ladder and landed with a breath taking thud on the cold clay floor and all was dark.

She tried to take a breath but nothing was coming. She fought to keep from fainting.

She swallowed hard and regained her breathing in time. The air was filled with dust and musk and she choked over on her side and put her hand to the pain on her face. She felt the warmth of wet blood on her shaking finger tips.

The clay beneath her cheek was cold and damp and she imagined it a bare grave in the dark as her breaths began to steady and the tears welled up in her eyes, washing the grit away.

She shook and cried while God took what was left above and swept it away with a wave as if it never mattered at all.

Parker leaned on the rail of the pig pen and watched the storm move across the northern sky far away. The hogs were just finishing the last of Charlie. They pushed a fingerless hand about in the mud between them in play. Parker turned and walked away heavy with worry.

Boredom for an aging warrior is like a disease. The impulse to ride, raid and spill blood was always there.

Always.

He pounded the sides of head with his large fist trying to get it out. He flailed about in the air as if fighting swarms of jackets, but it kept taunting him like a thirst that can't be quenched, a hunger unsatisfied, a maddening unreachable itch.

His words to Henry came back to him in echoes of laughter. You are that man.

You are a killer and it is expected of you to behave as such. Like a bird has wings, a bird must fly. He has no choice in the matter; it is what he does. There is no fault or judgment.

You are that man.

He stepped up on the porch of the ranch and turned shoving his hands in his civilized pockets looking about his world and what had become of him. He figured his gains and losses there.

I am a man, he said in his mind.
I am a warrior. I am a killer of enemies.

Bird and Henry rode through the tall grass as the rain pelted and soaked them through. Two funnels in the distance moved in closer and eventually joined together as one enormous wall of twisting deadly energy a mile wide or more.

Henry knew that Zee was in it. His only hope was that it got her before Poole did.

The rocks there in the distance sat and offered shelter, but at a price. They seemed to evoke a great weight that other larger rocks did not. Bird kept quiet and worried for he had not told the truth when he said the caves was forbidden to Henry. They were in fact forbidden to all.

His father had told him this and he had heard it all his life, but never asked why. There was suggested evil in the warning but never explained. Implications of ancient law and heavy spiritual cost were suggested but those words were never really spoken either.

Stay away, it is sacred, was all they said.

He had rode there many times and watched from the distant range and let the siren spirits tempt him, and now as they approached the foot of the rocks and the canyon of the lost, Bird was driven to know the truths of this place. He wanted at least a story of his own; an adventure that no other Comanche had, or at least lived to tell, that he could one day share and have it heard and passed on through his linage.

They climbed into the canyon and continued to ride. The sound of the storm whistled through the passes ahead of them and caused their ears to hum and burst. Henry pushed Jed at full gallop around the turns and bends and deep into the belly of this small divide.

Where there was life at the mouth in foliage and small trees. There was less inside and the further they went the more lifeless and dark it became.

Around a final curve and through a narrow path the rocks opened up to vast theater and they set the horses and looked at the hole in the mountains, so large that it could only have been made by the foot of God or the impact of a dead star. The floor soft and flat with a strange red soil barren of all of earth's nutrients and it closed in around the hooves of the horses and made them confused and slightly panicked.

The sky above was yellow and sick with jaundice and beyond that to the north, black and boiling violently.

Henry scanned the walls, hundreds of caves gapping their black moaning mouths at them while the wild sky churned. It was the ruins of a lost forgotten race, a stone city abandoned. He picked the nearest cave, one of the largest and headed toward it. Bird held back and marveled at the grand arena for a few seconds and wondered what history it held and then followed.

They rode through the mouth and entered what would be the first chamber and dismounted. Henry left Jed standing, walked back to the opening and looked out and cursed Parker and cursed his luck and entrapment, another delay. "Looks like we're here till it passes."

Then he said to himself, when I finish with Poole, I'm comin for you, Parker.

Bird petted and calmed his paint thoughtfully and watched Henry. "Henry Faro, what is this place? Do you know this place?"

Henry turned a little and said, "Just Henry or Faro. You don't need to use both names. Sound like a damn fool."

Bird walked up next to Henry and looked out across the great flat floor as well. "Do you know this place?"

"I've been here before," Henry said. "And yer right, it's a strange place, lots a ghost."

"Ghost? Jed said."

"Spirits. There was a great extermination here, lot a years ago, hundreds a years. The Spanish came across the sea and traveled up from Mexico, killed everybody and everything."

"Spanish..." Bird said. "I have heard the stories. Where did they come from?"

"A country, a tribe, far away and across the ocean."

"Why? They had done something to the Spanish?"

"I recon not"

"Then, why?"

"Why not? God the Devil, gold, put all three together and ya got all the reason ya need. Because that's what men do."

Henry thought about that after he said it, and the truth in it hit hard and nearly brought him down. He sighed and steadied himself against the rocky wall. "Feel good about it boy, it was yer people that drove them out, back into Mexico."

Bird said nothing but like Henry, he felt the sadness of the world all at once overcome him, the absolute hopelessness of the human race and the tragic effects of all its selfish convictions. He thought about his own people and the great change that had happened in just his life time. His mind was mixed with stories of the past and realities of the present in such a way that left him rootless and disembodied. The place was heavy with grief.

"Don't think too much," Henry said, turning and walking back into the cave. "It don't pay well."

Bird turned and watched Henry pull apples from his saddle bag and feed them to Jed. He patted his neck and whispered something in his ear.

Jed whispered back, kill him?

"Hush that up," Henry said.

"This man my father wants you to kill, you don't want to kill him, do you?"

Henry ignored Bird's question for a long time and continued to comfort Jed who was nervous and frightened of the cave and finally said more or less to himself. "I reckon I got it in me."

"For all the reasons you said? "

"Yeah, all those, some others too. Some history with him and me. Don't ya mind none about it."

Bird looked back out to the sky and took a deep breath and turned and walked back into the cave as well. He started gathering the sticks that were piled here and there and prepared them in a pit for a fire. Henry watched him out the corner of his eye, his dark shadowed figure, working, assembling the brush, his contorted red face had taken on new features.

When Bird was ready he reached into a pouch slung around his neck and produced a small amount of dried weeds that smelled of lantern oil and tucked it down in the center of the twigs. He pulled out of the same pouch a piece of flint and steel and held them down low and struck them together several times until the spark agreed and a small flame began to grow. He looked up at Henry and nodded and invitation. The flames cast light across his painted face and he sat back and fed the fire with a long gentle breath. He smiled like a devil in the flames as they grew.

"Is it that simple, Henry? Can everything in the world be that simple?"

Henry walked toward the fire slow and without an answer. He pulled his coat behind his pistols and crouched across from the young brave and just sat there staring into the fire. He searched it long and hard and finally looked up and said, "I don't know. No, there's nothin simple about it, nothin at all. And yet, it's as simple as sin."

Poole and his men stood in the rain and watched from the east as the twister swept in from the west. The good Reverend thought it a gift, a message, a sign and basted in its awesome glory while the other men pulled the hoods of their dusters and looked at one another. They wanted nothing to do with such gifts.

"The lord is please with thee," he said pulling his horse around and facing his men. "He sends unto us his assistance and approval that these lands must be cleansed. Have I not told thee we are blessed?"

Rhoar watched from his hood through the rain and the storm as this messiah made yet another speech of confirmation. A sick and twisted feeling had been growing in Rhoar since they first set out. He had witnessed blind vengeance before but had never fallen into it himself. Now it was awake and alive and its hunger pulsed in the grass and rolled in the clouds and ran with the wind.

It was real, alive and feeding. Rhoar turned in his saddle and looked back at the town as it burned. The wind pulled the black smoke rising off to the south and it streaked across the lower canvas of sky like the work of some hellish artist of the damned.

Both captivating and horrid the world was and all at once.

He looked back at Poole who finished his prayer and made a charging motion with his staff for punctuation.

Rhoar sat and watched. The men stole quick glances at one another. The fury of the Lord burned in their eyes and in their hearts and they followed their leader on. They were growing tired and crazed and Rhoar knew if any reasoning remained in one of them at all, that it was quickly fading.

For the sake of self-preservation Rhoar said nothing but watched Poole's' spine twist and slither while he rode and led them toward the storm. Something had been lost and all was wrong and Rhoar wondered where it began and why things had changed so drastically and yet no other seemed to noticed.

He thought of it as drowning. You wouldn't think it possible till in the middle of it, and then it was too late.

He saw the way the Reverend had been looking at him, watching him and he knew it was only a matter of time, when and where that he'd have to answer for his thoughts. He began to prepare himself for that moment of judgment for he had seen it enough times that he could play it out in his mind; a gentle swim, warm waves caressing, promises of salvation, followed by the sudden panic that the shore was too far away and his breath and strength had lost its capacity to save.

He knew he was well in those waters but he followed anyway, against every instinct to turn and vanish into the blinding rain. He stayed in the company of a smiling maddening enemy for reasons he knew not as he felt the shores of reasoning drift further away.

Henry could hear the storm rage outside and the earth shook and trembled. Dust fell from the cracks in the cave. Bird seemed to be in some deep meditative state for a short time and the horses were skittish. Finally he looked up from the fire as Henry was making himself coffee with the pot and cup that Zee had packed.

"I've heard my father say that you were dead Henry, yet you seem alive as any other man. What does that mean?"

Henry crouched down and lifted the pot from the fire with a gloved hand, filled the cup and blew on his coffee and tested it with a sip. He glanced at Bird and back in the fire. "It just means that I've shed a skin. I was pretty well known as somebody else for a spell. I left it behind. That's all it means. I changed. Put on a new face."

"A new face, and this man you used to be, who was he?"

Henry let out an irritated sigh and looked at the red faced boy across the fire but saw that there was no judgment in his eyes or his words. He retrieved a stub cigar and lit it. "Turns out dyin ain't all that dependable."

Bird nodded in agreement. "And nothing remains of this man, the dead one?"

"No. A lot remains. He's still here," Henry said and thought for a long time. "People will believe what they're told dependin on who's doin the tellin?"

Again Bird nodded in agreement. "I have seen this to be true. It must have been somebody very important who said you were dead Henry. My father believes it, still."

"Politician, Governor of the state of Missouri. But that just sounds fancy, doesn't mean all that much. Your father doesn't believe it though, he just understands it."

"I do not understand it."

"Yeah," Henry thought. "Sometimes I don't understand it myself. It's a kinda, chickaree."

"What is Chick...?"

"It's like a trick." Henry lifted a stone from the cave floor and held it out in his palm for Bird to see, then he closed his palm and shook his fist twice and opened it again, empty.

"Where did it go?"

"Still here, just can't see it anymore." He closed his palm, shook his hand and tossed the stone across the fire to Bird.

He held it in his hand and studied it. "My father, I think he is right Henry, you are dead and therefore cannot die."

"I wish that were true, but it ain't." Henry Stood and walked over to Jed and patted his hind end and looked out the mouth of the cave at the black day.

"I think it is true," Bird said. "Back at the creek in woods, I could not kill you. I could not fire."

"That was different. It's not the same thing."

"I have never frozen that way. I wanted to kill, but I could not. I was frozen like ice."

"I would a missed from that distance."

"You were not trying to kill me. I know that."

Henry looked into the deep black abyss of Jed's eye and saw his fish eyed reflection there.

"And the men in the canyon, you should have been killed there as well."

"You were there, and yer party."

"I was sent. My father knew you would be there. He saw it before it happened."

"Your father is wise in the ways of fighting. He guessed, took a chance, and I was there."

"My men shoot well, very well, and we had good position, but no, there was something else there. It was too easy." Bird shook his head at the fire. He studied it a long time while Henry studied him too and Bird continued. "When I was very young, before the big house, my mother sent me to my father's tent. I do not remember what for. But when I lifted the flap and went in, do you know what I saw?"

Henry turned and walked back toward the fire, hitched his hip, looked at the young man and bit his bottom lip.

"My father was laying down in sleep but above the ground, just resting there like a feather on the wind. And the smoke from his fire dance about in a way I had never seen. It took the shape of spirits I think and they walked about around him."

Henry listened, finished his coffee and threw the grounds in the bottom of the cup in the fire.

"It does not matter," Bird said, "I did not understand it then, but here, in this place and this talk of chick-a-"

"Chickaree."

"Yes." He looked about the walls of the cave. "Chick-a-ree, of life, and death. I understand that things are real and happening that we cannot see. But some men can, men like my father. I understand more."

"I'm glad somebody does."

"My father has very strong medicine, Henry. He can travel and see things that no one can see, and it is true. It is not chick-o-ree." Bird paused and looked thoughtfully at Henry. "The others think I have inherited this medicine through him, but I have not. That is the chickaree of my life. I am a trick."

Something in Henry urged him to encourage the boy, to tell him it was better to be like him than his father, for heavy lay the crown of knowledge and insight and if that man not turn out strong enough to wear such a crown, it could kill him in the worst sort of way. Parker was such a man. Bird was not and Henry could see that the boy thought it a weakness.

"It's a different world," Henry said. "Yer world is a different kinda world and it will make you a different kinda man than yer father."

Bird looked past Henry as if something was there and shrugged a quiet laugh. "I know this. We disagree on many things. But I feel he is more fit for my world than I am."

Henry wanted to compliment the boy and verify his wisdom, and disagree with him too. He didn't have a son and would never have one, and was now feeling that loss as they spoke. But a long stillness took the place of his words as he thought it over and decided, it was meant to be. That Parker had sons because Parker was meant to have sons.

"I believe you will kill this man," Bird said.

"Reckon?"

"Yes. Not because my father wishes it but because you must. I think it must already be sewn on the blanket of time. "

"That's somthin to think about, "Henry said, wishing to change the subject. "He's a very clever prey. It won't be easy."

"You will succeed. You are like the stone and cannot be killed. You are wrong about my father though. "

"How's that?"

"He knows you are dead. He knows the dead. I believe that you are dead too."

Henry turned around and looked at Bird. "Thinkin like that could get your mule in a ditch."

"We are a crazy people I think. All the people in the world are strange and crazy, and dead. It is not until we die that we are born."

Henry smiled at that. "Dead people have one peculiar attribute though."

"They do not know it?"

"They can't kill."

Bird shook his head no. "You are mistaken. A worthy spirit with much medicine grows stronger with each passing life. It carries that medicine with it through many worlds and many forms. This is what I believe."

"So they *can* kill?"

"Yes, long and slow and in many places over time. You have strong medicine, Henry, like my father. It is written and many have seen it. My father has spoke of it. He knows things of the crazy and dead. He believes you have great medicine. He knows you as a worthy friend and fearless warrior."

Henry grew impatient with this talk, adjusted himself and looked at the young man. "Listen, a man is worth what he believes he's worth, if he believes he's a worth a lot, he's likely to do lot of things. If he believes he's worth nothing, then he's likely to do... anything."

Bird thought about that and nodded at the fire in agreement. "I have seen that. But tell me, which are you Henry Faro? What do you believe of yourself?"

Henry thought for a while and came up with many things but none he cared to speak.

"Is it time to wear a new face, again, Henry."

Henry spit, "we only have so many faces, kid."

The wet cold clay of the fruit cellar floor kissed her cheek as the last of the storms tirade passed above. She laid there in the dark while the sun crept through the cracks in the door above and its intensity stung her eyes as she blinked them open.

She had dreamt while away, but it was scattered and made little sense now. She sat with her legs folded beneath her, wracked with pain and worry. She knew what was left of her life had been reduced to nothing by the God she had half-heartedly given her soul to some years before. It was his to do as he pleased, she would have said of anybody else, but she felt a seed of spite in her heart now and let it grow.

She moaned as she turned over, stood on her knees and rubbed her neck. It hurt to breath and she pushed gently at her ribs until she found the injury with her fingers. Just bruised she thought, but still.

She felt around for the shot gun and found it in a thin shaft of light just to her left. She pulled it and placed the butt firm in the earth and used it to help herself to her feet.

Standing there for a long time, clearing the cob webs from her mind, she felt her skull through her hair and the goose egg there from the door that slammed her down.

The cellar had filled with enough light for her to find the ladder and she reached out and grabbed a rung and steadied herself with the gun tucked under her arm. She climbed, slow and with difficulty and when she reached the door she knew it was going to be hard to keep the gun and push the heavy door up enough to get through.

Henry had dug the cellar by hand and built the door strong enough to carry the weight of his horses and cattle. She had always left it open while stocking or retrieving. She pushed with her hand first and nothing. Climbing another rung, knees bent, she situated her forearm flat against the door and pushed with all she had and the pain in her ribs shot through her like fire taking her breath away.

Zee relaxed, let the gun drop back down, wrapped her arms around the ladder and rested her head there; wheezing in a painful hurried breath and thought hard of another way. She was looking quite trapped and it might be a very long time, if ever, before somebody came.

She held on until her elbow began to cramp, and she started lowering herself back down when she caught the faint drum of hoof beats.

Stopping, mid ladder she locked her elbow around and listened and waited. They were coming closer and there were many and not the sounds she wanted to hear.

She lowered herself the rest of the way down and stood silent, listening.

They were nearly upon the ranch and she picked up the shot gun and backed into the darkness among the jars of jellies, jams, beats and apples where the suns light could not reach and waited for a familiar voice.

Goddamn looters, she thought, or worse. She stayed still in her corner and listened.

Poole's men circled around the wreckage of the ranch. The house had been lifted off its stone foundation and left in a scattered wood pile some hundred yards away or more. Clothes, furniture, lamps, shoes, pots and pans lay strewn across the acreage among the dead cattle and horses. A rooster walked about and picked at the ground as if it was all good and well.

The Reverend set his horse there in the middle and looked about with a disappointed air. "Leave not a stone unturned," he bellowed. "There is evil here and it's alive, I can smell it. Let it be known God's work is not finished and thee shall seek out these demons were they hide and cast them away into the fires of damnation. Search them out I say and drag them forth into the light of the Lords vengeance. Search, search. I want them alive."

The men began to dismount and scurry about. Rhoar was last to set foot on the ground. He watched the others for a time, lifting debris, laughing and going through personals. Packing their saddle bags with whatever they found of value or interest.

Slowly the group made their way to the whole of the house and continued their hunt. They rooted through papers and letters and stuffed the ones that were dry and clean in their pockets and saddles for toiletry later.

Rhoar walked over to the now empty corral and stood and looked out at the black range in the distance. He glanced off to his right and noticed a garden next to where the barn had been and walked over and crouched next to it. It was positioned in a way that caught the whole days light and he looked at what was left of the vegetables there. It had been picked clean recently for nothing was left but vines and soil.

He stood up and shot his eyes around the farm and saw Poole there staring back at him. "What is it, William?"

Rhoar thought about his answer for a long time. "Nothing," he said. "There's nobody here, Reverend."

"I will be the decider of such things. Keep looking. They're here." Poole turned his horse and his back to Rhoar and gave orders of burning to the other men.

Rhoar watched them all and when no bodies were found in the tossed house they emptied kerosene lanterns and gathered broken furniture, clothing and whatever else that would burn and set it all ablaze. Rhoar half-heartedly went about his search.

He turned and looked around the foundation of the barn. Its wood sides and roof lay stretched out far to the east in splinters of red. A carriage there mangled and ruined atop a dead plow horse. He stepped inside and walked the straw covered floor taking in the bridles, buckets, saddles and ropes and suddenly his footstep echoed back at him and he stopped. He looked down and scratched his boot across the wood and tapped it lightly.

Hollow.

He turned on his heels and stole a glance at the Reverend. His back was still turned. He kept his eyes on Poole as he crouched and swept away the straw and dust with his glove until he saw the large brass ring laying there. He stood immediately and his mind raced and his eyes darted about. A smart man would have a storm cellar in these parts.

Evening was setting in and it had been the longest day. Rhoar was sick and tired, spiritual afflicted past the point of recovery, sick of death, tired from killing.

He left the barn area in a roundabout way, walked across the ranch and joined the others as they stood in the glow of the fire. He listened to their talk but didn't offer any of his own. He noticed their casual way, hands in pockets, pulling on suspenders, talking of politics, God, wives, children and things and people and places of no direct relation to the day's events and their conversation were void of guilt or remorse.

He stole a glance back at Poole still sitting on his horse as the sun hovered behind swollen, tired and stressed. Poole's eyes closed, bible under his right hand as he read and turned the pages that lay in his twisted mind. Rhoar stole another glance past and across the floor of the barn, but did not keep it there.

How could he get past this place? How could he live past this? All the others were safe in faith, blind in faith, and he wondered as he looked among their faces just how far they would follow Poole without question. Did any other man here have the same doubts in their actions?

No amount of stolen money in all the world was worth this tax he thought, and there his faith lie and festered and it would most definitely bring about the end of him. He knew the time for following had passed and the need to act was drawing near.

He could almost feel the rope about his neck, Poole's steel in his organs. He tried to join in a conversation of volunteering to paint the Hotel Independence.

He finally prayed. But he prayed that whatever lay beneath the floor of the barn would stay there and stay still. God grant them wisdom.

Parker stood outside and studied the sky to the west. He smelled the air, the wind, for in it was prophecy. He read the clouds and watched the hawks that circled about in a confused pattern. He circled his hand in the air to the men, Bird's party, that stood watching, mounted and ready. He turned and walked to the sweat tent on the edge of the property as they all rode hard in formation with the sudden certainty of a lit fuse.

He pulled back the deer skin flap and circled the smoldering fire pit rubbing his chin in concentration.

He loosened and removed his tie and jacket hurriedly and tossed them to the side as he began adding wood to this perpetual fire. He dropped to his knees and fanned the flames until they leapt to a healthy and vigorous height. He stood and circled the pit several times more as he removed the rest of his clothing and closed the flap.

Parker was not a man to leave nature to its course. He gathered the pottery that held his paints from the side of the teepee and placed them near the raging fire to soften. Sweat began to leave his body and roll down his dark skin. His medicine bag, wrapped and tied, he held cupped in the palms of his hands and he lifted it to the sky as he closed his eyes and began his song, chanting and crying to the spirits of his ancestors and his enemies, the Gods of fortune.

His mind began to change, transform.

He sat in a lotus position and his eyes roll back under their closed lids as he lifted out of his flesh and bone and into the air, into the sky and into a hawk that circled waiting.

He blinked and opened his strange new eyes and he was in. He saw the teepee below, smoke seeping from the stitching. He saw the roof of the ranch and all going on there, a child looking up at him shaded his eyes with his little hand and waved with the other.

He left it behind and flew north with strong wings that carried him fast across the desert grasses and into the mesa's of the north.

And further away the curvature of the earth gave way and he saw the raiding party at the Faro ranch and the burning and looting that was taking place there. He opened his throat and cawed and flew over and around of them. Poole looked up from his horse and their eyes met and he saw in them the future that would be.

He made another pass, circling around and returned back to the south and flew fast and hard toward the sacred canyon with the forbidden caves and over it he became disembodied for a time.

This had never happened before and felt like a weightless falling until he found his way back.

When he did he opened his eyes and felt his familiar vessel and all the pains of age and battles past that it carried.

He emerged from the tent and his horse sat looking at him, waiting. They conspired together a plan for the deeds ahead.

They walked the horses from the cave and out onto the floor of the canyon. The storm had left an eerie silence in its wake. The sky noticeably effected, as were the rocks, the earth and the world, both seen and unseen. The sun hovered low in the west bruised and injured in an otherwise empty sky. Henry mounted Jed and looked at Bird. "You don't have to come."

Bird thought and looked at Henry with a steely determination. He climbed his paint.

"Suit yer self."

They rode across the crater floor and into the rocks the way they came. The horse's hooves now covered in red clay wet from the hard brief rain. Neither said another word and their pace was fast for lost time. The entered back out on to barren landscape and headed into the setting sun.

Henry had been afflicted with thought, memories of the past ever since he set out and left Zee behind. He had done it many times before, but never had he taken so much with him. Always it was a just job. Possibly he had thought about this one, too long, too hard, before hand and it had worn the luck off it.

But he knew it was more likely that he not thought about it enough, or in the right way.

This time, and Henry reflected on his departure, the days before, weeks, month's and years all leading up, Zee's eyes, the dream the night before of the river and bridge, the screaming faces, and they all began to look familiar now as he pushed Jed and rode on harder and faster.

There on the bridge, the men and women, he knew the faces of, children he'd seen before, all dead during the course of his life and all in one way or another, by his hand.

Bird was having the same afflictions of thought, but with the future.

As they rode together, these past and futures converged. The Indian had only known reservation life and he was beginning to realize it had not been a life of freedom but one of slavery and lies. His father was a great manipulator and had conjured a life there that was not real. Parker had traded his freedom for life, currency and legislation. He had sold his soul in a way.

Bird was educated and taught by a world that would never be his. His grandmother was white and while that blood ran through his veins, he would never know equality in that world. He had been sheltered under his father's illusions that their tribe was a race strong and flourishing.

He thought of the caves and people long dead and how it screamed of truth, and that truth was the same for him and for his father and would be for the rest his generation and culture.

He kicked the paint harder and harder as his face grew tight with anger.

Henry thought of the ragged traveler he'd come across outside Independence. The man had been close by in his mind ever since, walking along, dragging that broken soul through the dust, blind and lost. He wondered how far he'd traveled before realizing he was that far west. How had he survived through the states he'd crossed in that uniform forty years old without being shot dead or hanged for sport.

Resentments were thick from the war and probably would be forever. Henry had left his own clothing of the time behind, his face, his name, but that was all. He was the man on the road, the lost traveler.

He thought of the men he rode with then, now all dead or close enough. His brother, he had not seen or heard from now in many years. They would soon meet again he thought. They were all calling him through time.

Henry had friends in high political places. Pardons were given with conditions. He stayed behind and died, even went to his own funeral, and after they celebrated in the saloons of St. Joe they said their farewells, packed up moving West like pilgrims for paradise and found it there in Indian Territory.

Paradise.

Henry thought of paradise, the idea and the reality and the big empty between.

The grassy floor, thinning by the mile, moved by swift as time under the horses hoofs. Jed knew the way from here and all Henry had to do was ride and think.

He thought it a fitting circumstance he'd gotten himself into. It was deserved. Even Zee deserved it for staying by him all those years. She knew the man and what he was, and she quietly ignored it and went along as if they were proper and safe.

She held tea parties and went shopping and congressed in gossip with the wives of respected members of the church, most of which were all confederate sympathizers, their men, all of the Golden Circle and they talked secretly of rise ups and revolution.

She never missed Sunday meeting. Zee was a perfect accessory to many a crimes against man and nature, and as he rode he hoped she'd learned something along the way, something of self-preservation, some instincts, some cold bloodedness, for it was headed her way, if it wasn't there already, and she would need it.

Saliva streamed from Jed mouth as he a snorted and pushed through the miles. His legs began to burn and ache in a way that he'd never felt.

The young man who rode close in his flank was something else to think about. They had shared time now and Henry's convictions were growing soft in old age like an apple left to rot on a tree at the end of a season.

The boy deserved a favor though.

He should have killed him back at the cave and left him with his like. He should have killed him at the creek.

The boy was barely a man but his time had passed before he was even born.

The life that lay ahead for him would not be easy and he would grow old and bitter with disillusionment if he was unlucky enough to grow old at all. It was in this reasoning Henry thought that he needed to die. There would be no shelter of contentment for his race and for that, he was worse than dead already.

He was a bright boy and God would punish him for that.

It would be a mercy killing.

Twenty miles or more had passed and the tired sun was being pushed down by darkness. Bird's paint had been bleeding from the nose and suddenly tripped once at full speed and then again, and then his legs gave out altogether and its body skidded through the grass and dirt and lay heavy, gasping and dying from exhaustion over the boys leg.

Trapped as he was he laid his head back and breathed and looked about the sky as the paint took his last breaths.

Henry pulled back on the reins and brought Jed to a halt and twisted him around. He looked back at Bird trying to pull himself from under the dying horse. His rifle had fallen from reach and he felt his position in the clarity of truth as a grave one.

They had conversation but they were not friends and Bird's sudden compromised situation and the look on Henry's face only confirmed it.

Henry began to walk Jed back slow while Bird pushed on the dead animal and clawed for his weapon, pulling grass by the roots and grabbing stones to throw.

Henry seated Jed and crossed his arms across the saddle's horn. The young man's red painted face was pulled back in a defiant grimace. He let out a long deep breath and let the stones and dirt fall from his hands. "Well, go on, Henry Faro; kill me if it pleases you. And it would, would it not?"

Henry Glanced across the horizon and fixed his eyes back to Bird. "I won't take any pleasure in it. It's for yer own good."

Bird spit at Jed's hooves and Jed took a step back and snorted. "What are you waiting for then? Be done with it. It will be a good death for me Henry Faro and just another murder for you. We will not meet in the next life."

"No, I reckon not."

"Because you are a murderous coward, and your spirit is diseased with dishonor and shame. You are not a great warrior. You are nothing. You are a walking lie."

"Keep talkin," Henry said and drew his rifle from the saddle.

"Do you know why my father sent me, Henry Faro, do you know?"

Henry swung himself off Jed and walked toward Bird. He cocked the rifle and heard the cartridge slide into the chamber.

"He sent me because he knew you would fail. He knew."

Henry looked at the boy and the horse atop him wheezing blood over his words from his nose and mouth. Henry spit off to the side. "Maybe so."

"It's the truth. He knew you would not be able to kill this Rain King."

"Maybe," Henry said. "He sent you because he knew, *you* would fail."

Bird grit his teeth and panted with all the rage and determination of a trapped animal counting it's minutes of life left and his red face covered with sweat and desperation ran in streaks down his face. Henry could see the boys mind working, thinking, realizing. He could see it in his eyes.

Henry raised the rifle swiftly to his shoulder. "The world is changing. There's just no future in being an Indian. Your father knows that."

After a good and filling feast of the Faro's cow and chickens Poole gathered his men for evening prayer. The twisted broken house raged huge and hot with fire and the Reverend had placed himself in front of it for effect as he stood in the back of a broken wagon that he'd ordered righted.

"As my eyes cast upon the sight of the Lords will of the day, I cannot help but feel over joyed with our blessings."

Amen, they all shouted and raised their hands and guns to the sky. Rhoar paced slowly behind the wagon staying just out of the Reverends side sight.

"Where once was a land thick with sin, where Satan played with delight from within, has now been cleansed and born again. Into his graces we deliver, into his house he may consider, if the souls saved today can live for eternity in that way. God bless them. God bless them as we gather our wandered sheep this day."

They wailed, yes, yes, with eyes closed and wagged their fingers to the stars as he paused and surveyed his congregation from the ragged pulpit.

"Be not lost. Be not lost, for salvation comes with cost, and for those who tred in doubt, it is written, it is written, there is but one way out.

Out of the hell of the forgiving flesh must be through suffering and fire and pain and death. Only through these test can ye be reborn from eternal rest and dwell in the glory of the house of the Lord and taken into his loving nest.

Forever.

Forever, I say.

Forever."

The men were crying in their hands now, taking it in, shaking their head as the tears streaked down their soot, ash and blood caked faces there like gothic clowns in a an ancient tragedy.

Not since the disciples themselves had there been a group so faithful. And not since the disciples themselves had there been such blindness to the waste that lay around and behind and ahead in the history of man.

And Rhoar watched from behind and paced while his eyes shifted from Poole's shoulders to the barn and back again.

Judas he was and Judas he is. And he could feel it crawling from inside of him to the surface where all would soon see. He tried to fight it back, to swallow it down, to wash it away with the faith of the Reverend's words but it would not recede and it would not hide and he knew soon it would glow for all to see. He had to get away and it would have to be soon.

She had opened a jar of stewed tomatoes and sat on an apple crate turned on end in a corner and ate them with her fingers. The last of the days light died down now through the cracks in the door above and soon it would be pitch black in the cellar. She knew it would be a long time till morning and even longer till Henry came back if he ever did.

She held her children close in mind and heart and their faces would appear in the dark over there and over here and floating above and below and even when she closed her eyes.

Henry's face would be there too looking this way and that and showing its short gamut of expressions. His smile she liked the most for it had been years since she saw it. It reminded her of happy times when they were young and close and spoke to each other in a way that lovers do, with words that were true and from the heart.

She had forgotten most of them but she was sure they were said and the way they made her feel still lingered.

Even though it was summer she imagined the children now young adults going to classes and carrying their books and meeting with friends under trees for kisses and conversations. The weather was sunny and brisk in these scenes and the colors of that world were the colors of October.

The young men, clean shaven, scar-less and handsome wore heavy sweaters, and the girls all pretty and perfumed with the softest hair wore wool skirts, white shirts with flushed cheeks and lips of crimson. And they smiled and laughed and planned futures in bustling cities full of life hope and opportunity.

But Zee knew it was only a dream of hers, like that of a child that she most likely read about in a book or saw in a display or catalogue.

She always wanted to go there to the east where all was colorful and clean and the seasons were so spectacular that they alone were worth living for.

New England.

She never told Henry that she loved the idea of those two words.

But she sat there in her reality barefoot and ragged staring at the images in the dark and chewing like an insane woman in a cell with dirty fingers and coagulated blood on her head and face while a spider wandered through her ratted hair.

She would need water soon and she had none. She hated stewed tomatoes but Henry didn't. She would need company soon and there would be none. Love, soon, and there would be none.

She swallowed and glanced up at the door in the ceiling and wondered if she could get it open enough for a peek at the voices above.

It sounded like a great gathering and it was possible she was hiding from rescue. Crawling away to a certain death like a wild kitten from a kind and curious child with milk and bread.

It was possible.

She could hear Henry's voice; stay put and trusts no man in no man's land.

She was so tired of this philosophy, so tired of living in fear and danger on the fringes of the world.

She placed the jar on the floor and felt around for the shot gun in the corner and wiped her mouth on her sleeve. The dark was playing tricks on her eyes and mind and she knew and expected it but still it was hard to accept.

She stood and listened for a while but nothing coherent came of that so she reached out and grasp a rung on the ladder. She looked up in the darkness at where the door should be and saw only blackness.

Once away from the compound Parker's messengers split into three with four to the east, four to the south and four to west. They rode hard and fast and with urgency into the night and none spoke and none squandered their time.

Parker left his horse standing and went back to his fire and watched the world in the flames. He watched Henry and Bird there on the prairie floor as he dipped two fingers into a pot of black paint made from roots, berries and blood from some long dead enemy.

He started on the right side of his forehead and slowly pulled the paint down across his closed eye and over his cheek bone and down under his chin.

He began to sing his war song, quiet at first and then he placed his whole hand in the pot and his death prayer turned to a crying wailing scream.

And all those around looked upon his tent with fear and worry while his wives cried, clutching children in the dark windows of the ranch.

Parker pulled his giant hand from the jar and slapped his face and covered it whole with the bluish black face of death. And he stood before the fire and felt the power of warriors past fill his mind and spirit. Once again an appetite for victory was burning in him.

Henry pulled the trigger. The rifle kicked back hard against his shoulder. He caught the spent shell in the air as the crack rang out in the cold of the new night. The dying horse ended its wheezing and its head lay in the grass and bled as Bird looked at Henry, eyes bulged and heart pounding hard against his ribs, so hard Henry could hear it himself.

Jed had walked back to where they were and looked upon Bird with an almost amused expression. You are a hard number to figure, Henry.

Bird said nothing as Henry relaxed the rifle, turned his back and untied the rope from his saddle and let it drop.

He sheathed the rifle, bent down and fashioned a slip knot in the rope and dropped it over the horn on Jed's saddle and turned him around. He let the rope run through his glove as he walked back toward Bird and fashioned the other end in the same way and tied it tight above the knuckle of the dead horse's leg. Jed began to walk away until the rope was taught and the tied leg stretched up into the air and then he pulled and the body slid free off the boy. Bird sat up, examined his leg and rubbed his shin.

Bird looked at Henry as just a shadowed figure now in the dark as he pulled his knife from behind his coat. He turned toward Jed and cut the rope at the horn and let it fall. He lifted up the trailing reins, put a boot in the stirrup and pulled himself up into the saddle.

Bird stood and tested his leg. Neither man said anything. Jed launched off into a full gallop and Bird watched as they were swallowed by the night.

He stood there under a starry sky for a long time and listened to the world around and his world within and he smelled the scent of the horses sweat and death and the grass and the cottonwood trees from a nearby forest.

Some light sweet fragrance of blooming night flowers and their taste in the air reached his lips. It was good to feel alive and alone from anyone.

He breathed deep and was aware that it was a good and wondrous miracle that he existed at all.

He wondered why Henry did not kill him. Perhaps he too was already dead and therefore could not. There was nothing or no one near to say he wasn't. He tried to think of a time when he could have died and not knew it and there were many but none to be sure of.

Perhaps that is the way of dying, to leave one world and enter another where all is dead but none are aware.

He gathered up the rope with hopes of catching another horse and felt around with his feet until he found his rifle. He unsaddled the dead horse and

rolled the blanket across his shoulders, and with
his rope, rifle and water he set out guided by the
North Star just to his right.

Bird began to walk and think, and soon was in a
slow pacing trot.

Thinking.

He's just a man, Henry Faro, neither dead nor
alive but somewhere in between, like everyone
else. These rumors of a walking dead man are
rumors of design.

A blanket to hide under.

What was that word?

What was it?

Chickaree.

His father had told him once that all whites fear
death. Bird knew now it was not true. He had met
Henry Faro and in his eyes and actions he saw no
fear there. But he saw nothing else either, nothing
at all.

As the miles grew between them Bird began to
see Henry in a different way and he was aware and
it made him think of Henry as this mythical entity,
much the same way his father had spoken of Henry
on occasion.

When Bird was a child there were few whites
that his father liked to talk about or think of, but
Henry Faro was one of those few.

He knew his father feared no man, beast or
God. He believed it. But Bird wondered now while
running through the tall grass in the cool night air
as his heart pumped his blood through his limbs
like streams through a forest, if he did in fact fear

Henry Faro or this Rain King. And if he did, why would he deliver his own son into the company of these men of death.

These killers of killers.

Why wouldn't his father just kill them both and be done with it.

He thought it would be good thing to ask of his father when he returned. But he would also keep on and pay attention for tracks, clues or traces of that answer till he did.

There was more truth in finding an answer than hear one.

It was a game he thought, a serious deadly game. The only kind his father liked to play. But he would not believe his father sent him to be killed as Henry said. He knew his father and the way he worked and it was not his way.

The revival dispersed but the men mingled a bit and talked of the day's deliverance and right. William Rhoar assisted the Reverend down from the wagon. No one seemed to wonder or question their motivation anymore. It was as if a hunting party had had a long fruitful harvest and celebrations were earned. They began to make camps here and there, relax, smoke and discuss various passages of the Book in the fire lights. The wood and timbers from the house and barn continued to burn giving the night the look of a red day.

Rhoar leaned and gripped the wheel of the wagon and crossed his boots. Poole's eyes passed over his men and out into the darkness to the south. He turned and looked at Rhoar.

"It's been a good day, William."

Rhoar kicked the dust with the toe of his boot. "I don't think he's around. Even if it was him like that batty old bitch said. He's far into old Mexico by now."

Poole placed his hand on Rhoar's shoulders and looked above him at the smoke clouding the stars. "No, he's near, I can feel it. Feel his evil, feel his fear. No man can hide from the Lords vengeance.

He will be delivered to us for his just judgment. There's something here that he must return to... something, some one. You will see."

Rhoar let out a deep heavy sigh. A fiddle had broken out in the night, scratching a hymn on the air.

Rhoar began to turn and Poole stopped him. "I've been watching you, William. I've seen many times what can happen when a man has lost his way, lost his faith and walks within a darkened day. I can see more than you know, and what I've seen is beginning to grow. I will help you before it's too late."

Rhoar turned to Poole and looked out at the men in the distance. This was just between them. "Alright, you want it?"

Poole leaned in and waited. "Go on. "

"Cut the shit. You and me go a long way back, Poole. I know yer fuckin cracked and that's been all right with me. What's been good for you's been good for me."

Poole straightened himself and narrowed his eyes as if to turn Rhoar to stone where he stood.

"And don't even start that chosen one bullshit. I know you. But this has gone too far. Parker's horses were one thing, I never cared for injuns and he's as loony as you are. But burning whole towns, murdering women and children and dogs-" He paused a long time and shook his head at the ground. "We need to go back. We need to get the hell outta here and get back to the way things were. We are way too close here to somethin else altogether. I don't like. I just don't like it."

Poole studied the man's face in the glow of the bon fired house. "Go on. There's more?"

"I feel like were chasin the goddamn devil, Poole, and purdy soon, he's gonna turn round an bite us in the fuckin ass. You know this man, and so do I. He ain't nothin to fuck with. And if Parker finds out we're down this way; there ain't a God or man that can help us."

Poole contemplated his words but not for long and he put his hand over his heart and said, "you have nothing to fear so long as we stay on the path that God has chosen. Why now do you doubt me?"

Rhoar pushed the Reverend's hand away and gritted his teeth. "It ain't fear goddamn it, its common sense, somethin that seems to a left ya, Poole. And I have no doubt. It's not doubt. Ya just want that feather in yer hat. Or maybe it goes back farther yet, huh?"

Poole's mind wondered in the past for a moment and he looked out across the property and his men; some making their beds, some still scrounging, others brushing their horses, and yet others conversing and drinking coffee. Their smiles and relaxed postures before their camp fires spoke confirmation and he looked further out into the blackened ridge to the west that lay against the sky like the jagged back of a sleeping dragon.

He turned back to Rhoar and grasps his arms with affection. "Walk with me, William."

William took a deep breath, rolled his eyes and turned with the Reverend as they walked toward what was left of the burning house. Still massive as it was and the flames swelled at the ground and leapt high in the sky as it hissed crackled and moaned.

The heat reached them as Poole walked Rhoar away from the others with his hand in the nap of Rhoar's back. Rhoar pulled back a little and turned his head and winched at that searing heat now stinging his cheek.

"It was a long time ago," Poole said. "I had given my soul over to Him and he accepted it."

"I don't recon He wants it, Poole," William said and held a glove up to block the heat away.

"Let me finish. A long time ago and another life it was, a life of sin and without direction. A life that was no better than that of a God-less heathen Indian like Parker. That life I knew to be false and yet I lived it anyway and I drank and dined and danced with the devil's whores, and all the while I lived while Satan's hate burned inside of me with a wonderful seductive deceptive happiness that I never thought could be matched. Until, I met her. I met war."

Poole nudged Rhoar another inch toward the fire and raised his hands above and spread his long fingers over the fire and closed his eyes and played those fingers as if plucking some imagined heavenly strings.

"I was there too," Rhoar said.

"War," Poole continued. "Oh, the great cleansing machines of war." He pulled his hands back and kissed his fingers and Rhoar saw the flesh there that had begun to blister.

"I knew when I saved my first soul, I was all of twenty years of age and I saw the light leave him and the shadows that came and swarmed and consumed that light and swallowed it whole while it twisted and fought before my eyes." Poole leaned back and put his hands on his hips inside his coat. "I knew. William. I knew, the glory of God had revealed itself to me and in doing so had blessed me with a purpose in this life. And do you know what that purpose is, William?

William had turned to face Poole now, unaffected by the heat from the fire although he could smell singed hair of his white beard, and he watched with wonderment and furrowed brow as the Reverend turned toward him and smiled.

"You have lost yer fuckin mind," Rhoar said. "If ya ever had one at all."

Poole reached out and placed a hand on Rhoar's shoulder and then behind his neck as he pulled him closer to whisper in his ear and Rhoar felt the thrust of Poole's blade brought from his side and shoved in slow and with precision up between the center of Rhoar's rib cage and he twisted it until it found the soft quiet puncture of the heart.

"To cleans this world of sinners, doubters, and disbelievers in the name of Lord Almighty, Amen."

Rhoar's eyes teared as he struggled for his pistol and blood ran from his mouth in choking gulps but it was too late. Poole held him tight and close, upright by the knife as he worked it and placed his lips over Rhoar's and kissed until he felt the life leaving his body.

"Fuck, you," Rhoar spit, his final words and they seemed to few.

Poole leaned back and swung his head back and forth from left to right. "May God have *no* mercy on your damned soul," he said and he lifted and walked Rhoar's dying carcass up to the raging fire and dropped him there to burn.

He turned to walk away wiping Rhoar's blood from his mouth on his sleeve.

"Reverend Poole!" a shout rang out, "Reverend Poole, over here!"

There comes a time and it is often that that time is late. And when Henry reached the edge of what was left of Sanford he slowed and sat Jed before the destruction there and he knew that time was in fact far too late. He lifted his hat and wiped his brow with the back of his forearm.

The night was in its witching hour when all things of this world and the next are conspiring to blend. A soft warm breeze blew through the silent streets scattering articles of past lives, burnt papers, sunbrellas and rags of clothing.

Among the ashes, embers and fires still burning there lay the bodies strewn about in unrecognizable postures of horror. And it spoke of a place that God had forgotten, where a moon had no tide to order. And a sun had never set or risen to kiss a day.

Jed heaved, exhausted and barely able to hold his own weight and skittered nervously back and sideways as Henry dismounted in the middle of the street and kicked at a black dog feasting on a body there.

"Git, goddamn it," he said but the dog snarled viciously over his supper until Henry drew a pistol and it turned and tore up the street.

Henry leaned down over Sherriff Olson, a friend now fallen and disfigured in a heap of blood drenched clothing. The little whore Lily lay faceless, filthy and naked some fifty feet away.

Jed nearly collapsed at that point and Henry stood and patted his jowls. "Whoa boy, whoa."

He walked him to a leaning water trough but held him back by the bridle bit until he cleared the ash off the surface with his glove and tested it himself first by smell then a taste. It was clean and good and he let go and Jed drank between breaths.

There were miles yet ahead and Henry knew it would be dawn before he reached home even at a full run. Jed was spent. He was looking thin and mangy.

It could kill him.

He needed a fresh horse.

He looked around for signs of life. There had to have been some animals that had escaped this and they would wonder back in search of things they needed or knew. It was pitch dark away from the fires and spirits were haunting everywhere in the deceptive shadows and wisps of smoke.

He patted Jed on his hind quarter, pulled his rifle from its scabbard, leaned it against the trough and pulled the buckle that undone his saddle. He slid it off and dropped it in the street. Jed pulled his head up from the water and said, are you going to kill me now, Henry?

"No."

Jed rejected the idea of being left with a step back. Henry pulled him back with the reins and talked some sense to him. He unbridled him and removed his bit. Jed jumped and ran a few feet naked and free, invigorated with water and weightlessness. He stopped, turned and looked at Henry and said, which way to Wichita Falls?

"No," Henry said. "Ya did well and I'll be back for ya."

Jed knew neither was true.

Henry turned, untied the bag from the arrested saddle and slung it over his shoulder, heavier now than he remembered. He lifted his canteen from the ground, kneeled and filled it from the bottom of the trough. Jed took some steps in his direction and Henry stood and drank as the horse waited. I can make it, Jed said.

He lowered his arm and looked at Jed. "Fine then, ya hard headed sons a bitch. Go back, get the boy. Go slow and rest. Go find that Indian and take him home. There ain't no hurry, ya hear?"

He filled the canteen again and hung it about the horse's neck. Jed's giant eye blinked and Henry saw his own reflection there bowled and distorted. We don't need him, Jed said.

"I'm gonna need more than that. Take him back to Parker. He'll know. Go on now."

Jed turned and began to trot back south. Henry watched as he disappeared in the darkness and heard him begin to gallop. He shook his head and shouted, "walk, ya stupid ass."

He picked up the rifle and held it firm as he advanced down the street with caution, looking listening. His stride was odd and off balance from riding so long, but had fixed itself as he reached the edge of town and he stood before a great mass in the darkness yonder. The only thing not burning and shifting with living fire and he made it out to be the train. The great promise of prosperity and deliverance now silenced for a time but it would be the only thing that would live again.

The sound of hooves galloping reached his ears and he raised the rifle in that direction.

Zelda heard the shouts, fell back down the ladder and scurried to her corner. She'd gotten the door open a crack and stole glances about her home and the activities above. She knew she'd been found out.

She felt around the shelf for the box of shot gun shells and spilled them out, shoving as many as she could down the front of her dress. The brass was cold against her breast and she pulled back both hammers and tucked the butt up under her arm. She patted it tight into the clay wall behind her and aimed it upward and waited. All was silent as an eternity passed, plenty of time for her to cuss her own stupidity and allow her mind to fill with panic and terror.

Her breath heaved and left her body in hard raspy chugs as the door slammed open and the cellar filled with a lighter shade of darkness and the air was fresh and clean.

A torch dropped down to the floor and flooded her grave with light. She shielded her eyes until they adjusted and looked at the fire and felt her throat harden. Her tearing eyes shot back up at the open door. She had a sure target now in a hatless head that poked down. The torch light cast red upon his face and beard and she saw his eyes looking straight at her. She pulled both triggers and that face was gone. She felt his warm blood covering her face and arms as the rest of his body fell in onto the floor extinguishing the torch.

She breached the gun and pulled the hot spent shells with trembling fingers and reloaded and waited. She heard the talking and shouting above as they conspired their revenge of their fallen brother and planned their next assault.

She waited and cried and looked at the body there and that hole in the earth above it, all she could do was wait.

The men above grew silent and their footsteps ceased to shuffle after a while. She prayed to her God that they would just leave. She prayed for Henry to come, guns a fire, and kill the whole lot of them dead, sending them to hell or worse. She prayed for his reassuring words and his safe and tender embrace. She prayed his lips would touch hers again and he'd run his gentle fingers through her cares and wash them clean of this nightmare.

She prayed and prayed, and as time fell the silence grew and she was overcome by a drumming in her head and her faith wavered and weakened to whimpering pleas.

She broke- and tears poured from her eyes with blinding salt and Zee knew her prayers would not be answered. She knew they never had been. She could see her crying children. She could see her unborn grandchildren. She could see Henry's body hanging from a noose in a tree in a lost and lonely meadow.

The barrels of the gun were heavy and pulling her down. Her arms were tired. Her hair lay wet and stringy with blood and plastered against her face.

And then a deep bellowing voice from above, familiar and yet forgotten and it said, "Zelda?"

She felt her body flush and her blood run cold.

Over five miles Bird ran in the night without stopping, slowing or changing his pace. His bad leg burned with pain. His side hurt and occasionally he would bend to stretch and pick up a thought stone to rub and take his mind off his limitations.

His mind and body worked together like a perpetual engine. His only map was on the sky and the sounds of the world were of the world inside him, the sounds of his heart drumming in time with his breathing, his blood pumping. He would switch his Winchester from hand to hand to keep his balance.

He knew not what lay ahead but was making good time in getting there.

And he ran through the pines and across the prairies and into the Black Mesas of no man's land where the earth become hard and loose under his feet. Through canyons and over the creeks he stayed on Henry's trail and did not stop to even drink.

At some point he tried to keep track of time and distract himself from the pain by counting stars or thinking of stories told to him. Times when the Indian wars were an everyday affair and his father was a fierce and indestructible warrior and many would follow him to the spirit world with loyalty and conviction.

He had watched his father change colors like a threatened lizard and adapt to these new times and even prosper and profit in them. He left his old skin behind and all that it was, like a changeling.

He had witnessed how a man could die and another take his place. He saw this in his father and knew this was the way of Henry as well.

He was angry with his father as a child and felt then that it was a dishonorable activity to wear the white man's suit and to build a house that could not move with the seasons. But it seemed to him now that it was a necessary transformation and there was no defeat in it.

Is it more foolish to live in the world the Great Spirit has created or to die a death of reminiscence?

He thought he would speak of these things with his father if they ever shared time again and he would tell him of his new understanding of the world in which they had been left with.

For the first time Bird began to see his own future much different than his past and promised himself when this quest was through that he would set about filling the pages of that future not with contempt but with vigor enthusiasms. He would learn, adapt and better himself for this new world. He would not settle for Henry's words that he had no future.

He would build one.

Along the edge of a shallow cliff he stopped for the first time since he began, resting against his rifle with a hand on his knee while his breathing stabilized and the sound of his heart calmed and cleared from his ears. Nearly twenty miles he figured and he eventually began to hear again, hear the wind and the patter of his sweat hitting the thirsty rock beneath him.

He stood up and watched the day break the horizon in the east with a pale blue sliver painted on the sky and behind the shape of a horse standing on the rocks far away and looking back at him.

He knew it to be Henry's horse from its height and stance with his ghostly white coat glowing in the morning sun. He felt the chill of great despair sweep over him.

Three were killed in getting Zee from the cellar before morning. Poole tried talking her out first but with no success and not for long. He ordered men down in a rush until she could no longer keep up with reloading. Soon they dragged her out by the hair into the twilight of morn and the pain from their kicks and fist were lost on her as her eyes took in the unfamiliar world that was now hers.

Overcome as she was with the devastation of her land and home she tried to cover her privates as they ripped her clothes from her body like wet paper and stomped her head and limbs with the heels of their boots.

Poole raised a hand and they stopped their kicking and stretched her out on her back by her arms and legs while she cried and writhed in agony. He kneeled down close to her filthy hair, matted face and said, "good morning Zee. Guessing you remember who I am?"

Her pale breast bruised and scratched in the morning chill filled with air as she blinked the dust from her matted eyes. "Fuck you." She spit and regained just enough strength to struggle a few seconds more before she threw her head back and fell limp and gasping with exhaustion.

He smiled and wiped her spit from his face. "I will take that as confirmation. And then there is little doubt that you would also know why I am here."

Racked with pain she tried to speak through her throat but only whimpers and broken words came out. "Henry's left, left me. He's... dead. Ass-hole."

Poole drew in a deep breath and shook his head in doubt. "I do not believe that to be the truth."

She began to shake and cry. "True, it's true."

"You lying, whore." He screamed. "Now tell me true what I wish to hear."

"I... I, don't..."

All had left her and she clenched her eyes tight and searched her mind for a prayer and place to hide, a place of forgiveness, a prayer of peace and numbness, and the only prayer that came to mind was one for her remaining time here and that that time would be brief.

Poole stood a boot on either side of her rib cage while the men pulled at her limbs, laughed, grinned and groped at will. "On this day," he began, unbuttoning his trousers, "I hereby baptize thee, Zelda, Faro." He looked down. "It *is* Faro now, is it not? Yes, yes. That is the name I have heard. And a fitting one for the house of cards ye has built to dwell in. Poole reached a hand in and continued, "in the name of the Father, the Son and Holy Spirit, I baptize thee, Zelda Faro, in the name of our Lord," he smiled pulling it out and relieved himself over Zee's bare breast and then directed it on up to her face and she choked and spit on his urine there as the new day's sun sat low and swollen just above the horizon.

He finished shook, closed himself back up, leaned down on his knees and said to her, "Amen, Zee. Amen."

Poole stepped over to her side and instructed the men to let her go. They did, and she curled in a convulsing fetal position, choking and clawing at the dirt, pulling herself away slow and with little hope.

He reached down and grabbed a fist full of her hair and tightened it around his fist and pulled her to her knees as he walked slowly across the barn floor dragging her along.

Then men slapped and kicked her bare behind as if prodding a heifer into a pen. One man had pulled his belt and screamed his favorite passages from revelations through his gritted teeth as he whipped fiercely at her back and legs. She rolled along while others squeezed and grabbed at her flesh and shoved their hands and fingers in anywhere they would go as they hideously drooled and laughed.

Poole dropped her in the center of what was left of the corral and made them stand down.

He pulled his knife.

Zee made a last frantic lunge at a man near who had turned away. She pulled his pistol before he could stop her. The gun fired as she yanked it free and sent a bullet up through his throat as he staggered backward and tried to stop his own death with both hands clenched around his neck.

He fell to the ground and kicked until he was through.

Zee sat there on her knees catching her breath with a crazed snarled face.

Poole looked at the dead man there and around at the others ready to pounce as if they had somehow failed him. He looked at Zee and said, "Zee... put that down here." He pointed to the ground as if ordering a dog to sit.

She pulled the hammer back and held it out in front of her. It was heavy and she was weak and she saw her choices were few and clear.

Poole gave a signal with his eyes to a man coming up behind her and she saw it as well. Her brow rose up and tears began to fall again as her life played out fast before her and she tried to put all that was good in one place to keep and take with her.

She saw the chamber out before her with five bullets left. She shot at Poole and missed but went on to wound three others in her quick gunfire.

Acting fast with one shot left she put the barrel in her mouth and pulled the trigger. She sat balanced dead for a time before falling face first in the dirt.

Henry knew.

He felt it strike his soul like a great black hammer. He suddenly felt like a lonely fool in a crowd where he had been found out and all turned to look upon his foolery and this worth-less man staggering stupidly like an odd and awkward son, a freak of stupidity.

From the white stallion he had captured on the edge of town and ridden hard from night into morning toward home, he knew.

He stopped, pulling hard on the reigns and looked out into their future gone and could see her smiling face there in front of his eyes. All her emotions and mannerism played before him like a moving picture of her life and his. Her voice came on the wind as a favorite forgotten melody and nothing would be the same and nothing would ever matter from this point on.

She was gone and would only be in the folds of his mind, and only as long as that lasted, and then gone and forgotten from the history of time forever.

She was never before her time, and would never be again.

He sat for a long time and grieved a goodbye under the heavens that seemed to close in around him. The horse neighed, snorted and fidgeted in confusion. He reached down to his saddle bag and raised the flap, reached in for a handful of wadded notes and held them down in his lap. The wind blew and a single bill took flight and danced up and away like a butterfly with a broken wing.

He watched it go until it fell to the ground and tumble away. Never had a wage come with such a cost. It all seemed so foolish. He had not planned well. He had not considered all in those actions. He had performed the act many times before and with the same reckless preparations and it always worked out in the end.

What happened? Where was that moment when his instincts had failed him?

It did not matter now.

The end, the end, he thought. Therein lays the difference. The only plan he had made was that it would be the last plan and it would end there.

And in that only definite intention the wheels of time were set in motion to make it so, and so complete that he knew he had no choice in any matter anymore.

He saw it in his mind's eye. The end was waiting and he would see it through. But not with hands rose in a sure defeat. He would have his say in all of this, and he could, and he knew how.

He spurred the horse hard and changed his course and headed east into the morning sun.

Bird approached Jed with caution there in the Glass Mountains. He squatted down a few yards away and spoke softly to him while Jed munched on fauna that had managed a life from a crack in the rock. He asked of Henry and their journey and why he had come back and not gone on to his home. There was a message in the canteen around his neck, the removed saddle and rigging that Bird could see but Jed would not speak it. He would only raise his nose to the south in nudging gestures and walk in place.

Bird stood slowly and placed a hand on his nose and looked into his eye. He pulled the canteen off and drank and filled his palm for Jed. He put the canteen over his shoulder while the horse drank and walked around his side and slid onto his bare back.

He tried to coax the horse north but Jed kicked and rose up and Bird gripped his mane with both hands and kept his seat. Bird spoke to the horse and told him what they must do and there would be no argument about it and he tried again to turn him, but Jed jerked his head and started down the mesa toward the prairie floor to the south.

He removed himself from Jed's back and raised his arms in anger. "Go then, stupid horse, go."

He turned and starting walking away but stopped and looked back when he reached the place where they had met. Jed had followed him back up and stood close and insisted with a bite and a hard nudge against Birds head. Bird raised and waved his rifle and tried to shoo him but Jed only pushed him harder and turned away and waited.

Bird held his face in his hand while he thought of this peculiar behavior they were having. If his brothers could see him arguing with this stubborn horse they would laugh.

"What is it?" he asked Jed. "You came for me, this is true, but there is more."

Jed showed his impatience and kicked a shower of dust at Bird with his hind leg. He turned, snorted and charged the young man. Bird was nearly trampled but had spun to the side just in time and slammed the butt of his Winchester into Jed's flank.

Bird squatted there on the rock and studied the horse. Jed turned and faced him, calmed himself and looked into Birds face and soon Bird could see the futility in going north and could see the devastation that lay there.

Jed spoke at last and his words came through their minds. He told him it was too late for all of that and that another plan had been made and that he would carry him there.

Bird spoke to many horses before but none had spoken back that he could remember. Perhaps he had not listened in the right way.

Jed said, we have to go to your crazy father.

"Alright then," Bird said and stood. "That is what we will do, horse."

Bird stepped swiftly and mounted Jed again and left his hands free while he climbed down the rocks to the high plains and broke into easy gallop south.

Henry traveled fast along the border and through the killing fields of horses in the mid-day sun. The rotting carcasses had color now in the light of day and that gave it no improvement. He could see where they were seasoned with flies and maggots while hawks vultures and crows dotted the plains and the skies. This new horse took no interest in such things and continued through unconcerned.

Henry wished for the night, eternally.

By evening he had reached the eastern timbers and followed the trail through the pines and oak that he remembered before. It was not a road and it had not been traveled since his last pass there.

At the base of a Red Cedar and nearly hidden by dead brush sat the blind soldier with hands in his lap, swollen and bloated. His eyes stared upward with a look of astonishment but he did not move and he did not inquire. Henry sat the horse and saw the man had walked his last mile. He dismounted and kept the reigns close as he walked over and squatted down before him.

"So we meet again old yank," he whispered more or less to himself.

He made quick careful search of the man's pockets and found nothing but holes. He placed a glove on his chest and felt the hard iron beneath his coat. He respectfully reached in and pulled the pistol out and studied it, confederate issued, rusted beyond use and empty.

"So old pard, it seems we have some more things in common."

He sat there looking at the old man's face for a long time as if expecting something and when nothing came he dropped the reigns of the horse behind him and returned the pistol to the man coat, closed his eyes and stood.

"I spect we'll meet again," he said and turned walking the horse a ways before mounting and riding on.

When they reached the camp he had made in the tall grass by the river, there was no obvious indication that anyone had been there before, but he noticed the little things he'd left and a good scout would see it in the same way.

He looked out at the forest wall to the east and then through the cattails along the bank and across the golden fields of wild wheat to the north that rose up the hill on the other side and flowed like a golden silk sheet laid to dry in a warm breeze.

That bridge up river stood quiet and shadowed and whistled out a melancholy song with the wind through its trestles as if calling the slow current with a promise of a destination.

He walked the horse down the soft bank and into the water where he could quench his thirst and sat there, listening, waiting. He could smell rain in the north and death in the west.

He spurred the horse up the hill, across the fields, passed the great white canvas of their holy camp and into town.

He walked the horse slowly down the main street. Women and children were all that were left and they darted into buildings with their ghastly expressions frozen on their faces. The birds fell silent and dogs tucked their tales and stood stupid and confused.

He must have been a frightful sight, he thought; filthy, ravaged and worn.

Henry sat the horse at the old hotel, lifted his hat and wiped his brown with his sleeve.

With silence all around, he stepped down and let the horse go where it pleased.

The rain came on the third day and Poole took his thanks from the men there at the Faro Ranch. He waved his staff at the heavy bellowing heavens and they bust open with a warm cleansing shower that stayed and punctuated their mission. They danced, gave prayer and drank from the sky.

They had eaten all there was to eat and burned all there was to burn. Zee's body had been mounted on a cross fashioned from barn beams and erected high for all to see as the last burning embers below her spit screamed as they died out from the drenching rains.

Hawks and magpies dove in and out carrying her flesh away for their young. The vultures had not yet found her.

All knew by then that Henry was not coming. They broke camp that evening when the rain had let up and lumbered slowly back east like a wandering tribe of hell's gypsy's, barely remembering what they came for.

Far in their place and in their minds from the comforts of civilization they rode and only conversed with themselves and their God under the stars and out into the vast open high plains.

Poole had taken refuge in a pulled wagon, repaired and covered, for he noticed an affliction come upon him that morning and the congregation might have noticed his weakness if he rode.

They didn't notice, but instead considered his covered distance an elevation in status, a reward.

At this point I am compelled to speak with you on the matters of this story, my story. Do not be alarmed, we will return soon enough and you will see why I've stepped forward this way.

There is not a thing in this world I tell you now that is stronger and more dangerous medicine than religion. I have seen it.

Mine eyes have seen the glory of the coming of the Lord. And he is trampling out the vintage where the grapes of wrath are stored.

Battle hymn, they call it. And truer more passionate words have not been sung or spoken.

But a man must walk with caution dealing with so called truths. They can be deceitful and destructive and they will take all if you are willing to give it.

Wide and far are His swarms and far from worldly consequences are judgments and sentencing or His killing and conquering.

It is said the world was given on to us to share and harvest in necessity and survival, but in religion it is not so. All of nature must be owned and divided into parcels and boxes and only available by those and to those deemed found and saved and worthy under the cross and coin.

It is not so much the fault of man as an attribute. A man must breathe, so he takes a breath. He must drink, so he drinks. He must have, so he have's. And when he must kill, he kills.

A man must dream for what he does not have, cannot have. For beyond each acquired dream lies a greater dream, a promise of fulfillment and happiness. And around it goes, like a dog chasing a tail too short to catch.

He searches the darkness out there where it does not exist. The thirst and hunger come from within and only there can it be quenched and fed.

I am late in my years now and have seen the passing of time here long enough to know that I need nothing that I was not already born with. I can take nothing with me from the world that it is not willing to give. All things are borrowed and only for a time.

I have learned to consider myself blessed with a full stomach and a good fire and the learned mind of knowing this. This knowledge did not come easy I tell you. I had to see a lot before I could truly see.

But even after all I've witnessed I do not know whether to thank The Great One for my long existence or to curse him for what he has allowed me to endure.

I do not know.

Henry stepped up the stairs of the Hotel. He pulled his pistol, looked around the empty streets and went inside. The clerk had dropped down below her register and was hiding but Henry could hear her breathing. He stood before the grand lobby, emptied of furnishings, and vast as a desert. He admired the woodwork on the staircase and the interior balconies that circled above. All well-oiled and rich with color, a contradiction to the buildings weathered exterior.

He walked toward the main desk and passed by, stepping around the side and pulled the hammer back on his dragoon. He kicked the swing gate open. She sat there on her knees, old and with her trembling hands raised. Her eyes watered from their heavy lids and in a voice that was high and childlike she pleaded, "no, no..."

Henry was not in a mood for mercy. He leveled the pistol to her head and fired, stepped through the gate and fired again. She stayed still in her fetal position, her face spread out on the floor in bloodied pieces.

Outside they heard the shots but people stayed behind their windows and hid in their homes.

He holstered his weapon; stepped over her to a dirty wood plaque of skeleton keys on hooks, some, the brass polished and new while others hung worn and tarnished from years of wear. The numbers were hammered in tags tied to the keys by braided horse hair and he selected one off the top row of a room in the back.

He passed through the gate again and stepped up to the register book, turned it around and flipped through the blank pages there. He lifted the quill from the ink for reasons unknown to him and scribbled across the whole page, *Poole* and turned away.

The stairs creaked under his weight and he took a mental note of the complaints of each one. When he reached the top he looked over the balcony to the lobby below and appreciated the view once again.

Making his way down the hall to the number on the door of the key, he stopped outside and placed and ear to the wall and heard nothing, nothing at all except the wind outside and a dog barking in the distance with long pauses in between.

He turned and kicked the door down of the room across the hall from his key and walked in. Tossing the key and his rifle on the bed he went to the window, standing off to one side and looked up the empty street to the south. There was no sign of life save the dust funnel that swerved back and forth in the empty street. Black clouds were coming from the west rolling slowly in over the land.

He looked around the room and the furnishings there. Odd artifacts, a skull and black candles placed about on the tables. Tarot cards scattered across the floor by an overturned wheelchair. The faint smell of burnt sage lay under that of musk and jasmine.

He crouched down and lifted a hand full of the cards from the floor and remembered his mother would play with such things in the dark of night when the world was sleeping. Henry would watch from a secret place as she either clapped with glee or cried or whispered and argued with the cards. He let them drop from his hands and stood.

In a small heap behind the door was the body of a woman rotting that he did not smell at first but now was coming to him, strong and putrid.

Other than the cat sized rodent feeding off the corpse, all was very quiet.

Sliding off his coat he stepped over the cards to a hall tree by the door and hung it up. He lifted his hat and hung that as well, turned and righted the wheelchair. It creaked and moaned as he rolled it over to the windows, sat and comforted himself crossing a leg.

Across the street, the Independence Savings and Loan stood closed, barren, broke. He patted his shirt pocket and looked for what was left of a cigar but it was too short for good and crumbled beyond use.

He had some tobacco left in his leather wrap, enough for a large cigarette that he rolled slowly, licked the paper, set it to dry on the arm of the chair, and held the stick match waiting.

He thought about Bird and Jed out there in the big empty and doubted the horse had made it back to Parker's. He knew Comanche as the finest bareback horsemen that ever lived and he had probably rode him to death and took another.

He picked up the cigarette, struck the sulfur tip of the match with his thumbnail and brought it to life.

He sat, smoked and stared at the bank below as the sun sat down in the west.

Bird did not approach the ranch right away but stood at a distance and watched the goings on there.

The inverted stars that lay on the roof seemed to turn in the last heat of the evening. Too far away to make out who, but more horses and men, more than could be counted filled the property, and their camps in their making, scattered around for miles in all directions, told of the many different tribes that had come.

A great congress, he thought, the end of the Rain King maybe, a false celebration.

He felt ashamed. Embarrassment swept over him. How could he ride in and admit his failure? What would his father say to him before these celebrators?

Jed was apprehensive as well and preferred the distance even though he was thirsty, tired and hungry and could smell oats and corn in the air.

They decided to make a fireless camp and wait till late in the night when most were sleeping. He never saw his father sleep more than minutes at a time so there was no fear of waking him.

He slid off Jed's back and sat on the ground and waited and watched. He had no blanket and it grew cold when the sun bid its farewell and went to bed for the night.

Jed had lain down on his side like a dog sleeping, something Bird had never saw a horse do except when lame or dead. He was good horse, smart horse, Bird thought, but kept the idea of keeping him as his own away in case he heard it.

He hunched up under Jed's breast and wrapped his arms around his knees and took advantage of the warmth of the horse's underbelly. He could hear Jed's heart pump fast and steady and it was a warm comforting place to be and soon Bird slipped off into a hungry dream.

When he woke the moon was high and the dream was real and it took a minute for it to run away and hide where dreams hide. Bird stood and looked out across the Parker ranch soaked in moonlight now and saw only the livestock that lived there. The hundreds before had left so quietly and without warning that he wondered if they were ever there at all or just a trick of the mind.

Jed climbed to his feet as well just seconds before the hoof beats were upon them. Bird turned and raised his rifle but the shadowed rider came fast and hard and its darkness swallowed up the sky and cloaked out the horizon.

As they traveled across the high plains toward home, Poole and his congregation settled into a state of spiritual nirvana. So right they were in their mission and so sure in its action that the moon seemed to flood them now with a heavenly light of warmth and acceptance.

They had truly done well for God and nature and secured their place in his kingdom for all eternity.

None had asked or even thought about William Rhoar. It was as if he never existed. No one thought of the bank teller, Phillips and his family. No one thought of their savings still out there. And no man, save for Poole remembered Henry Faro.

But Poole remembered, and it weighed on him there in the wagon while he closed his eyes and tried to rest. It haunted him through the night. He knew if Henry was alive he was not in Old Mexico but very close instead.

His fever worsened and made it difficult to connect his thoughts.

It was not fear or even concern that nagged at the Reverend but a feeling like that of an annoyance; a missing button, an untied shoe, a hole in a fence. Some *thing,* of such little importance but threatened to deliver consequences sooner or later.

He knew if Henry had not already retuned to the ranch, that he would, and then he would continue back to Independence. He would come for him and Poole played it out in his mind. Things left to say. Things left to do.

His body poured sweat in the cool of night and his skin burned with fire.

He knew Henry could travel faster and farther, a single man on a single horse, than they were traveling now.

It occurred to Poole, that what was eating at him was not the return of Henry but the comfort of the congregation. A few were ex-soldiers and hired guns but they were aged and Poole thought of them as tired and lazy. The rest were farmers, clerks and weak in courage and lame in the head when it came to killing.

They had grown comfortable with the idea that this was over and they had won something.

His stomach spoiled and bowels leaked. He relieved himself in the wagon where he could.

He thought back there in the dark of his years and travels as the wagon rocked and lumbered. Their progress was slow, gnawing and fed his impatience.

All things that made up the memories of his years, days, hours and minutes in this world would not leave him be and he flung himself in his fever from side to side in the wagon and swatted them away like flies at a feast of an empty table.

He screamed and fought the air and clawed at the faces in the darkness coming in in waves and receding away like mist in the wind only to return again.

The men heard it all but walked their horse on with no or little thought of what was going on in the wagon. Their minds were flooded with the approval of God and their thoughts were of warm beds, hot meals, wives and children waiting.

Things so distant they seemed more like wishes.

Henry slept in the chair by the window and wept in his dreams for they were filled with sadness and horror and regret. In dreams and only in dreams could he weep and grieve. It was in that place where there was no sky or floor or articles of God's distraction to appreciate living in some small way and justify loss and move on away from it and on with life, a fashioning of worth and optimism.

Only in dreams, could he be reduces and defeated in such a complete way that waking might feel like renewal and he could find the strength to stand against forces great and many in the real world without fear of failing or outcome.

Only in dreams, lies the true gravity of existence.

It matters not, what we do in this wink of a life, for all is lost to time. And only only in the waking world are we truly asleep and seduced with the gifts of sin. What is the world outside our selves, but a collective idea.

That is not a question, for it has no answer.

His eyes opened slowly in the dusky light of the room as the ticking of the comforting clock behind him faded behind the commotion outside in the distance, growing nearer.

He took a deep breath, felt the pain of his travels and prepared to deliver again, one more time, his own gifts of sin.

The stairs at the end of the long hall creaked as they did when he walked them.

He lifted the Colt from its holster and let it rest on his thigh. The door behind him opened slowly but he felt no urgency to act. A woman in the street below hurried a child by the ear away and into the mercantile.

"Hello Brother," Poole said.

When Henry did not respond Poole stepped in and to the side of the room and watched as he moved around to his far side and turned his head in a curious way.

When he had a better view he pulled the hair back behind his ears and shook himself all over. "I sssee the yearsss, have been, good to you. Baby brother."

Henry looked down at the pistol in his hand and pulled back the hammer slow as the chamber rolled against his pant leg. "Yer no brother of mine."

Poole smiled, shook his head at the floor, "mother loved, *me* more. Isss, that it?"

His brain was pounding with fever and his lust for blood barely in restraint. He placed his hand behind his back and felt the bone handle of his knife there and looked at Henry again. "We ssshould, cele-brate brother. The Lord hasss, deee-livered usss, again."

"There is no Lord, and yer just a false prophet with a fancy handle," Henry said and closed his eyes and laughed a little. "The Rain King. Who woulda thought. Just a nother fuckin carpet bagger."

He leaned forward, breathing hard and wringing with sweat and laughed. "Well, let usss, not tell anyone, huh?"

"Yer reign is done, Rain King.'

He shook his head again and furrowed his brow on Henry. "Isss it Zee... that whore?" he laughed. "You ssshould thank me. You are free from that, burrrden."

Henry watched the window as citizens began to gather in the street and converse.

"Isss, it the money you ssstole... from me? Keep it. Again, you ssshould, thank me. It brought us together. I wasss one of those, beginning, to believe you, dead. You ssshould thank me, thank our Lord, and sssavior, for your, resurrection."

Poole's words came as if he was pulling them with great effort.

Henry finally turned his head and looked at his brother's eyes, red and bouncing about in his skull, his grin rotted and yellow, his hair and clothes, filthy, stained with blood and drenched through with sweat.

Henry could smell the stench of death from his breath and it filled the room and burned his nostrils and turned his stomach. "I should, brother. I should thank this Lord a yers for showin me what a fool he is in puttin you on this earth. I should. But I'm not. I'm just gonna to kill ya instead."

Poole straightened his back, pulled his knife and his faced turned fierce as he screamed. "Kill me, kill me? You cannot. I am the truth, and, the, the wayyy."

"I should a done it years ago."

Poole narrowed his eyes and shook his head. "You are thief, murderer. And you, judge, *me*?"

Henry bit his bottom lip and agreed. "I am those things, but I never claimed to be somethin I'm not. I ain't never been fake. I never been a fake, anything. You are the same brother, but ya hide like a coward. Yer a fraud and a fake and any Lord who might be up there knows it and has left ya a long time ago. Left ya with yer fools to grovel at your feet and prop ya up." Henry laughed and raised the gun. "The king of fools they will call you in Hell."

Poole screamed, enraged, and marched toward Henry with deliverance as Henry pulled back on the wheel of the chair, turning, firing, putting Poole back a step with a slug in the chest, but it only slowed him and he came forward and Henry fired again. Poole caught it in his left side and it filled his coat with blood and flesh before he deflected Henry's hand and the next shot shattered the window as they fell to the floor. Poole pushed the blade in deep through Henry's chest and he let out a satisfying sigh as he did. Poole grinned and froth leaked from his lips over Henry's face.

Henry relaxed his body and looked up into his brother's face and watched those eye lids twitch and flutter as him whisper scripture.

They laid together awhile as they did as children, keeping one another warm on the winter nights when the winds were wild and blowing through the thin walls of the Missouri shack where they lived as family.

Poole lifted himself off Henry and stood panting, sweating, and weak with fever and leaking blood on the floor. He watched his brother in his final moments with no feeling or sense of his actions.

Henry could feel his lung filling with blood and drowning him. He turned his head slightly to see Livius dragging himself through the door and all the light and color of this world went out for a short time in Henry's eyes.

And then freedom.

And it came from a pin point in that darkest of darkness and swept in with a sudden flash.

Henry woke in a strange way and coughed, turned on his side and leaned on one arm and rested there. He felt no pain, either from injury or age. None of the sadness or despair which had plagued him longer than he could remember existed in his mind or heart.

He could hear the wind and the soft rustle of tall grass all around. The current of the river behind him ran and danced across rocks in the shallows under a gleaming bridge of light.

The sky above had never been so vibrant and blue with wisps of clouds sailing slowly by like soft white schooners of fortunate travelers.

And through the sun lit wheat a child-like laughter came forward and Zee's pretty face parted through the reeds with warmth in her smile and love in her eyes.

Young again, angelic and clean.

She turned about in a dress of cotton and lace and whispered with a hurried excitement. "Henry, come with me. I want to show you."

Henry smiled at her, as he rose to his feet. And he followed her as they ran, danced and played through the fields and away.

On the last day, in a bone colored dawn, Poole gave his sermon. He had been patched and made to live but was still sick with fever and all could see his weakness as he leaned against his pulpit slurring his words.

They prayed for him, with him and *to* him for his full recovery. His sermon was short with great long pauses where he just stood and looked crazily about their worried faces.

A celebration had been planned after, a great feast across the bridge and among a grove of willows that lived there.

But as they exited the church, two by two and prepared to make their way, all stood still as the trees in the field outside and gazed up along the crest of the hill.

The wind was pushing a storm in behind us and a few drops of rain patted my shoulder as I watched them all standing on the prairie.

I was there, on the best horse I have ever known, and at the side of my father, his face painted black for war and death. And one thousand Comanche, Pawnee and Apache braves at our flanks filled the swaying golden waves of wheat.

Poole looked up and saw us there and knew. Thunder broke across the sky as my father raised his rifle overhead. And we, and the rain, rode down hard and fast with wrath on Independence that day. And in when it was through we left nothing for man or beast to say it ever existed at all.

ENJOY OTHER BOOKS
BY
KEVIN LYNN HELMICK

Clovis Point

Sebastian Cross

Heartland Gothic

Driving Alone
&
other tales from the outside

www.ingramcontent.com/pod-product-compliance
Lightning Source LLC
Chambersburg PA
CBHW032048240626
47154CB00003B/1134